'I'm sorry for blubbering all over you.'

'It's okay.' His fingers slowed as something in his gaze changed, heated. Her breath caught.

The hand at her jaw moved back, curving around her nape, his thumb settling against the underside of her chin. He used it to apply gentle pressure to tilt her head further back.

His gaze settled on her mouth. Oh, man—was he going to kiss her?

Unable to stop herself, she licked her suddenly parched lips.

'Molly…'

The word was whispered. A statement, not a question. But she heard the request nonetheless.

Dear Reader

One would expect a seasoned traveller to love the adventure of flying from place to place, living in lands far from home, learning about new cultures and different types of food. That's me! All except for the very first point: flying from place to place. During my adult years I've lived outside my home country more than I've lived within its borders. That means I have to fly. A lot. And you know what? I tremble every time I step foot on a plane.

My father—a man I look up to—spent his life around planes. He served with the Hurricane Hunters, a group of brave souls who fly into hurricanes gathering information. And later, during his time with the Navy, he worked as a flight mechanic aboard an aircraft carrier. He still loves planes. I should have inherited a little of that love, right? Nope. My husband still has to grip my hand during each and every take-off. What would I do if I were *married* to a pilot? That simple thought led to DOCTOR'S MILE-HIGH FLING—the story of a rescue pilot and the doctor who works with him.

Thank you for joining Blake and Molly as they experience the joy and heartbreak of working under very difficult conditions. Their dedication to their patients helps Molly overcome her fear and rise to meet each new challenge. Best of all, this special couple finds love along the way. I hope you enjoy reading about their journey as much as I enjoyed writing it!

Sincerely

Tina Beckett

DOCTOR'S
MILE-HIGH FLING

BY
TINA BECKETT

MILLS
BOON

First published in Great Britain 2012
by Mills & Boon, an imprint of Harlequin (UK) Limited.
Harlequin (UK) Limited, Eton House, 18-24 Paradise Road,
Richmond, Surrey TW9 1SR

© Tina Beckett 2012

ISBN: 978 0 263 22875 5

Harlequin (UK) policy is to use papers that are natural, renewable and recyclable products and made from wood grown in sustainable forests. The logging and manufacturing process conform to the legal environmental regulations of the country of origin.

Printed and bound in Great Britain
by CPI Antony Rowe, Chippenham, Wiltshire

Born to a family that was always on the move, **Tina Beckett** learned to pack a suitcase almost before she knew how to tie her shoes. Fortunately she met a man who also loved to travel, and she snapped him right up. Married for over twenty years, Tina has three wonderful children and has lived in gorgeous places such as Portugal and Brazil.

Living where English reading material is difficult to find has its drawbacks, however. Tina had to come up with creative ways to satisfy her love for romance novels, so she picked up her pen and tried writing one. After her tenth book, she realised she was hooked. She was officially a writer.

A three-time *Golden Heart* finalist, and fluent in Portuguese, Tina now divides her time between the United States and Brazil. She loves to use exotic locales as the backdrop for many of her stories. When she's not writing you can find her either on horseback or soldering stained glass panels for her home.

Tina loves to hear from readers. You can contact her through her website, or friend her on Facebook.

This is Tina's second book for
Mills & Boon® Medical™ Romance.

Check out her exciting debut,
DOCTOR'S GUIDE TO DATING IN THE JUNGLE,
available from www.millsandboon.co.uk

To my two greatest heroes: my father and my husband.
I love you both.

CHAPTER ONE

A FINE line existed between taking a dare and actually going through with it.

Molly McKinna was about to cross that line. Belted in and ready to take off, she glanced out of the window at her partner in crime, who simply made a rolling motion with his hand: get on with it.

Easy for Doug to say. His clammy fingers weren't the ones glued to the sides of the copilot seat of the small Cessna.

Flying. Why did it have to involve flying?

"Are you ready?" The flash of a hard dimple signaled the rescue pilot's amusement, but he could laugh his head off for all she cared. As long as he brought her back from Dutch Harbor alive.

She agreed with Doug, really she did. She had to decide if she could hack the flight from Anchorage to the Aleutian islands before accepting the job. But why did she have to choose a location where the only mode of transportation involved whizzing across the ocean as if shot from a giant slingshot?

You'd think being born to a bush pilot would give her an innate love for flying. But since her father, a man with thirty years of experience, had died in a plane crash on this very same route while she'd been in medical school, she no longer had much confidence in the whole flying scene. In fact, she'd avoided it ever since.

And yet here she was. Desperation sometimes bred stupidity.

Realizing the man at the controls was awaiting her reply, she mumbled, "Do I look ready?"

Either he didn't hear her, or figured that was as close to an affirmative answer as he was likely to get, because his mouth quirked once again before he revved the engines to a howling fury and raced toward the end of the tarmac.

Oh, God, oh, God, oh, God...

Then they were off the ground and climbing fast.

She only realized her eyes were screwed shut when her traveling companion's deep voice broke through the whine of the engine. "You can let go now."

Cracking open one eyelid, she glanced sideways and encountered the pilot's strong tanned jaw, the lightest dusting of dark stubble making him look more human somehow. When she'd first arrived at the airport, he'd seemed a little annoyed at being recruited to fly her to check out the medical facilities on the islands. Moments later, she'd decided she'd either imagined his reaction or he hid his emotions all too well.

Even so, she couldn't blame him for being irritated, since he'd wound up having to watch and wait while Doug had given her a pep talk about cars being more dangerous than planes. Not that his speech had helped calm her racing heart!

No way could she run now, though. She was strapped in and hanging high above the sea. And she still had the return trip to look forward to.

"So the flight takes three hours?" Molly forced her hands off the seat and into her lap, linking her fingers in what she hoped was a reasonable facsimile of casual indifference.

"Depending on weather conditions, yes."

"And today's conditions are...?"

"For this time of year?" He slid a sideway glance at her and raised his brows. "About normal."

Normal.

Molly gave an inward eye roll. Well, that certainly gave her a lot to go on. Why did every pilot she'd ever met speak in that deep soothing baritone that only made her want to scramble for the nearest life vest? Did their final exam include an "octave" test or something? Were the pilots with high squeaky voices ejected in mid-flight?

Her teeth came down on her lip. Okay, the words *ejected* and *mid-flight* were officially banned from her vocabulary.

"I'm sorry about your father." He looked straight ahead. "He was a good man."

"You knew him?" That surprised her—enough to let her push aside some of her fear. She'd seen the hunky pilot around the hospital from time to time. She even knew his name was Blake Taylor, but her father had never mentioned him when he'd been alive.

Maybe someone had seen fit to enlighten him. The accident had happened four years ago, but the people in charge had laid the blame squarely in her dad's lap. They felt he'd been reckless to attempt to fly during that storm. As did her mother. It infuriated her to no end. Most of her friends knew better than to bring up his name in her company. Then again, this man wasn't a friend, neither was he likely to become one. And if he said one ugly word about her father, she was going to—

"Wayne helped train me. In my opinion." His voice trailed off.

Molly's backbone stiffened further. Was Blake aware of the circumstances of the accident?

A hand came off the yoke—how had she even remembered that word?—and touched her arm. "I think he made the right call to fly that day, for the record."

"Y-you do?" It was chilly inside the cockpit, and the heater struggled to keep up, kicking out a lukewarm stream of air.

But the touch of the pilot's hand heated her instantly. "That's not the prevailing opinion, from what I've heard."

Not even her mother had cut her dad any slack, nagging him relentlessly to give up flying—to get a job closer to home. Her bitterness at his refusal had aged her, tilting her mouth permanently down at the corners. Once Molly had returned from medical school, her mom had focused that vast reservoir of neediness on her only daughter, urging her to live at home. Between her mother and her ex-boyfriend, those two years in Anchorage had sucked the life from her, left her feeling suffocated and alone.

Then a job had opened up in the Aleutians, and she'd leapt at it, flying or no flying. Her mother's reaction to the news still rang in her ears: *Go on and get yourself killed. Leave me all alone. You're just like your father!*

Was she?

Heavens, she hoped so. Maybe that was another reason she'd needed this job so very badly. It was not only a means of escape but a way to hang on to a little piece of her father.

She glanced out the window. The more altitude they gained, though, the more she rued her decision as an impulsive lapse in judgment. But the alternative was untenable. Staying at the hospital had been awkward at best, disastrous at worst. Besides, her father had loved his job, had said he couldn't imagine doing anything else. Maybe she just needed to make peace with that—to try to understand what had motivated him to keep making these trips.

Blake smiled at her, breaking into her thoughts. "Don't listen to them. They're all too happy to shift the blame to someone other than themselves."

She had to blink a few times to realize he wasn't talking about her mother but about those who blamed her father for the accident. "So not everyone thought my father was at fault?"

"Ask a few of the local pilots. I think you'll be surprised at their answers." He paused. "The weather over the islands can be unpredictable even during the summer. One minute it's clear blue skies, and the next…"

"So why do it?" Maybe she should be asking herself that very same question. "Surely you could have been an EMT or chosen something safer than this? Alaska Regional could always use a few more paramedics."

And not one of the single nurses—or any of the married ones, for that matter—would complain if he hung around the hospital a little more. Blake was something of a legend around that place. But from the whispered comments she'd overheard, none of the women in question had managed to worm their way past that charming smile and into his bed.

He shrugged. "As a kid, I loved watching old videos of Evel Knievel. Since I can't rocket across Snake River Canyon, I figure I can fly from Anchorage to Dutch Harbor. All I lack is the cool jumpsuit."

"Evel Knievel never successfully jumped that river."

"But he tried."

Molly shuddered. She hoped he wasn't drawing an analogy between the famous daredevil's doomed flight and the one she was now on. Did she really want to work with a man who seemed to be hooked on adrenaline? She didn't have a choice, since he was considered the best of the best now that her father was gone. Accepting this position meant she'd fly with him from time to time as they medevaced patients from the islands to the hospital in Anchorage.

If she took the job.

Nothing was set in stone. In fact, she couldn't risk jeopardizing the project, if she couldn't get past her fear. She'd have to let someone else take her place. Except none of the other doctors had stepped up and volunteered—they all had families, and no one was anxious to leave a thriving hospital to work in a government-funded clinic.

And part of her father's heart was still on those islands. A part she wanted desperately to understand.

She blinked, realizing the stabbing terror that had frozen her on takeoff was trickling away. She was still afraid, but the more Blake talked the more her nerves settled.

It had to be his voice. Maybe flight instructors gave lessons in hypnotism as well as voice modulation.

"What about you?" he asked. "Are you seriously thinking about taking the position? Forgive me for pointing out the obvious, but you don't seem to be in love with the idea of flying."

Was that his way of calling her chicken? The urge to flap her wings and cluck had only happened once so far, during takeoff. "Maybe I need to understand why my dad traveled back and forth between the mainland and the islands. To make peace with where his journey led him."

No need to tell him she was a coward in more ways than one. That sometimes it was easier to run than to stand your ground and fight.

He was silent for a minute, before he answered softly. "You can't always make peace with it. Sometimes all you can do is accept what life dishes up and then move past it."

Or you could always fly away from it as fast as you could.

The plane dipped for a second and so did Molly's heart. "What was that?"

"Just a pothole."

"Sorry?" The fear was back, stronger than ever. She licked her lips, trying not to focus on the vibrations of the plane around her but noticing every tiny shiver just the same.

"Turbulence. It's like bumps in a road. You wouldn't expect to have glassy-smooth highways forever, would you?"

"No, of course not." She relaxed her grip on the shoulder harness.

He was right. It was just a pothole. Not even a very big one.

Somehow thinking of it like that made it easier. "My mom hated flying. She never went to the islands with my dad, no matter how many times he asked her to. Not even to take a vacation. She wouldn't let me go either. And after his plane went down, she became even more…" Demanding? What exactly was she planning to say? "I just don't want to be like that, you know?"

"Understandable. But if your mom didn't let you fly with him, then when did you…?" He frowned. "This isn't your first time up, is it?"

"No!" She bit her lip. "Well, not exactly. I mean, I've been on a plane before."

He scrubbed a hand through his hair, the dark silky locks falling neatly back into place. "Really? When was the last time you were on one?"

"A few weeks ago." She tossed her head as if it had been nothing special.

He seemed to relax in his seat. "Where'd you go?"

"Go?"

"On your flight."

"We, uh, didn't exactly go anywhere." The mumbled words sounded weird even to her.

"I don't follow."

She hesitated. If she didn't tell him, he'd just ask Doug why she'd acted so whacked out during the flight once they got back to Anchorage. "The plane was part of a desensitization course."

Something she'd needed to make sure she could survive this trip.

"A what?" His head jerked to stare at her. "You mean you've never flown before in your life?"

Indignation washed over her. She had, but why should it matter? It was ridiculous to expect everyone to have flown all over the world from the time they could crawl. "I have flown. Just not recently. I—I couldn't."

Not since her father's accident.

"Oh, hell."

She shifted in her seat to face him. "What's that supposed to mean?"

"It means if you're looking for a pilot to help you get past your fear, you'd better keep looking. A desensitization expert I'm not." He laughed and the sound was no longer low and mellow. "I know of at least one person who'd testify to that fact. Only she's no longer speaking to me."

The anger behind that last comment made her hackles rise. Had he purposely scared someone during a flight? If so, he was right. She didn't want him flying her anywhere. "Fine. Once we get back to Anchorage, I'll make sure you never have to—"

"Wrong. Those 'bumps in the road' I mentioned? They're going to get worse the closer we get to the islands. And the landing strip at Dutch Harbor is barely up to FAA standards." He glanced up as if sending a distress call to some higher power. "Listen, I signed on to take a doctor to Unalaska to scope out the work at the clinic. I'm not here to be the next rung on your twelve-step ladder. If you expect me to sweet-talk you into getting back on the plane tomorrow, you're out of luck."

Her chin went up. "I guarantee that's not going to happen."

"You're right. It's not." His dark eyes swept over her face and the expression in them chilled her to the bone. "If you're not on the plane, strapped into your seat, by eight o'clock in the morning, you can find yourself a new pilot."

* * *

Okay, so he could have handled that better. A lot better.

But from the moment Blake had noticed her clutching her seat, a warning siren had gone off in his brain. He'd quickly dismissed it, chalking up her reaction to takeoff jitters. A lot of people got nervous, especially on flights to the Aleutians, where landings could be very hairy. Transitioning from a jet engine to a turboprop seven years ago had given him a few gray hairs of his own, so who could blame her?

Besides, her dad—a man Blake had looked up to and respected—was famous in these parts, so he'd had some ridiculous notion that Wayne McKinna's daughter would have logged some serious flight hours. Her physical appearance had only added to that impression. Brown, choppy locks were cut in a way that gave her delicate face a fearless impudent look. And the bold, take-charge style drew immediate attention to her eyes. Green. Intelligent. Framed by incredibly thick lashes.

She looked ready to take on any challenge that came her way.

Desensitization classes. *Great.*

What the hell was she doing, taking a job that involved medevacing patients to Anchorage?

Even Sharon hadn't been that afraid of flying. And yet her constant nagging to move back to the mainland and to switch to flying passenger jets had proved to be the final straw in an already disintegrating marriage. Wayne had understood exactly where he was coming from, said he'd fought the same battles with his own wife.

Blake loved the island where he'd grown up. Loved the challenge of landing on that tiny airstrip in Dutch Harbor.

Sharon hated both.

After the divorce, he'd decided no one would take those things away from him. Not again.

He glanced over at Molly. She was furiously staring out

the front window, her arms folded across her chest, her full
bottom lip thinned.

You can find yourself a new pilot.

The fact that she'd answered his outrageous declaration
with silence told him everything he needed to know.

He'd blown whatever chance he might have had with her.

If he'd even had one. The woman probably had men doing
penance laps until their knees bled, hoping for a chance to
go out with her.

He'd noticed Molly bustling around the ER over the past
year as he'd checked on some critical-care patients he'd flown
in from the islands. Her cheery attitude and gorgeous smile
had attracted his attention immediately. When someone had
told him she was the daughter of the late, great Wayne Mc-
Kinna, what had started as a tiny spark of attraction had
caught and held. She'd been away at medical school when
her father had shown him the ropes, so they'd never been officially introduced. By the time he'd realized who she was,
she was already spoken for. Besides, he was from the islands,
and Molly appeared to be very much a city girl at heart.

As he'd found out the hard way, oil and water might flirt
with each other for a while, but they eventually separated.

He should have reminded himself of that fact and kept
his distance.

Then she'd broken off her relationship and signed up for
the new health-care position the government had opened up
in the Aleutians. The temptation had been too much. He'd
juggled his schedule so *he'd* be the one flying her to the islands. Hoping he was wrong and that they might not be so different after all. Surely Wayne's daughter had vestigial wings
hidden somewhere under that lab coat—the love of flying
must be bred into her.

Wrong.

His jaw tightened. When would he learn? He should swear off marriage forever.

But he eventually wanted a wife. A family. Just not with someone who wanted to crush who he was and remake him into someone completely different.

That need went both ways, however. If he expected a woman to love him as he was, she had a right to expect the same.

Could he love a woman who was afraid of flying, who might end up hating the islands as much as his ex-wife?

Not a chance—he'd already tested that theory once. But that didn't mean he had to be an ass about it.

"Hey, listen. About what I said—"

"Don't worry. As soon as we land, I'll be out of your hair."

"Let me hook you up with someone I know who can fly you back. He's totally safe. Doesn't take any unnecessary chances."

"I'm a big girl. I can take care of myself."

She might be all grown up, but the quiet joy that had caught his attention at the hospital was gone.

Reaching over, he touched her hand, marveling at the softness of her skin. "Molly, we haven't got off to the best start here."

"You think?"

"I just didn't expect Wayne's daughter to be…"

Was there any good way to finish that phrase? He didn't think so.

"You didn't expect her to be what? A wimp?"

"I wasn't going to say that." Well, not those exact words, but the meaning was still there. "Knowing how your father died, it can't be easy for you to get back on a plane."

"Good thing you won't have to deal with *that* problem any more, then, isn't it?"

He waited for her to finish chopping him to bits, but Molly was evidently done, and rightly so.

Before he could figure out a way to smooth over the situation, the plane bucked, then settled back into place. He glanced out the cockpit window, realizing their heated words had diverted his attention for the past several minutes. Not good, because they were heading right into a long line of clouds stretching from side to side.

A front.

And an ugly one, from the look of it.

Molly threw him a panicked look, and Blake tensed.

There'd been nothing in the weather reports to indicate rough conditions today. But he knew things could blow up out of nowhere in this part of the world. This wasn't exactly the way he'd hoped the day would go.

But then again, when did his plans ever fall smoothly into place?

"Make sure your harness is tight."

"Why? What's happening?"

"See those clouds?"

"Yes."

"The little bumps in the road we've experienced are nothing compared to what's coming up." He glanced at her, adrenaline already beginning to spike through his system. "It looks like our smooth highway is about to turn into one oversize construction zone."

CHAPTER TWO

A SIREN sounded somewhere inside the plane, but Molly was too busy trying not to throw up to open her eyes and look around her.

They'd been bouncing around for what seemed like forever. How much more could the tiny aircraft take without coming apart at the seams?

Her fingers gripped her shoulder strap, the nausea from the turbulence almost overwhelming her. She breathed through her mouth, but didn't try to talk, too afraid she'd distract Blake and cause him to make some kind of fatal error.

Like her sniping and complaining might have already done.

Why hadn't she just sat back and pretended she was heading for the warm sands of the Caribbean with a handsome man? Because she was done pretending. Done going along with what others wanted her to be and do.

Maybe he'd report her.

To whom? The Brotherhood of Wronged Pilots?

Pilots probably had to deal with frightened passengers on a regular basis. Molly had just never dreamed she'd end up as a prime example of one.

He could report her to anyone he wanted, as long as he got them through this storm in one piece. And if he couldn't...

She swallowed the bile that rose higher in her throat. Her mother would have one more loved one to bury. Just like she'd predicted in that last rant before Molly had left the house for good.

Scratch that. They'd never found the bodies of her father or the nurse he'd been travelling with.

If Molly and Blake crashed into the ocean, theirs probably wouldn't be found either.

The siren cut off. Chancing a glance to the side, she noted the way Blake's hands fought with the controls, and she hurriedly shifted her attention to his face. The sight there wasn't any better. The muscles in his jaw stood out in stark relief to the rest of his features, his eyes narrowed in fierce concentration.

That had to be a bad sign. The man who worshipped Evel Knievel was worried.

Are we going to crash?

She kept the words to herself, but they repeated over and over inside her head.

The plane plummeted for several gut-wrenching seconds, before righting itself and climbing back to its previous position. Her stomach didn't follow suit, though. It was still dangling somewhere beneath the aircraft.

A mass of multihued gray bands seemed to scrape along her window as the plane plowed through the middle of the clouds. She flinched at each new bump and shimmy, expecting to be sent tumbling headlong into the sea at any moment. The fact that they were even high enough to be swallowed by clouds surprised her. For some reason she'd thought they'd be cruising well below them. "Don't worry. I've flown through worse." The tight words swirled around the cabin as if they too were caught up in the boiling turbulence outside.

Her hand went to her stomach and pressed hard. He'd flown through worse? An alarm had sounded, for heaven's sake. How much worse could it get?

A gust of wind shoved the plane to the right before releasing its grip. She couldn't hold back the question any longer. "How much farther?"

"We're about a half hour out. We can't land until the weather clears a little."

"Can't we climb above the storm?"

Another blast of air kept Blake from answering her for a minute or so. "Cessnas can't fly as high as commercial jets."

"Oh." Molly decided it was in her own best interests to let him concentrate on flying rather than having to field a constant stream of questions. Besides, there was always the not so off chance that her voice could transform into a high-pitched scream that would end up killing them both.

Better to maintain silence.

Between stutters and bumps, she studied him, finding that concentrating on something other than the conditions outside the plane helped keep the nausea and fear at bay. At least, partially.

Blake's hands were strong, his long tanned fingers gripping the controls. He'd shoved the sleeves of his black sweater halfway up his forearms, exposing lean muscles that bunched and released as he worked to steady the aircraft. Her eyes followed his arm up, curving over substantial biceps before she reached his shoulder. Broad. Taking up his space and some of hers in the tiny cockpit.

Reliable. Competent.

She couldn't see his eyes at the moment, but knew they were deep blue. She'd watched them go from warm and balmy to icy cold in a matter of seconds. Much like the weather outside had done.

Unfortunately, just as she was about to move her attention to that thick head of dark hair, he turned, catching her in mid-stare. "You okay?"

"Oh, uh…yeah." She scrambled for an excuse. "Just seeing if the view from the side is as horrible as it is from the front."

Ack! That hadn't come out right. "I meant the view outside the plane. I wasn't talking about you."

Maybe trying to explain herself wasn't the way to go.

She caught the flash of white teeth as he turned to face the weather again. "Well, that's a relief."

Forcing her attention back to the front windshield, she noted that the wind was calming a bit, along with her stomach.

Thank God. Maybe it was almost...

Suddenly, like a bullet exiting the barrel of a gun, they shot through the clouds and came out on the other side. The fierce turbulence vanished as quickly as it had started.

The contrast between dark and light was so startling, she was forced to squint as the sun peeked in at her and glinted off the nose of the plane. Once she regained her equilibrium, she sat up and drew a slow, careful breath, making sure she was still in one piece. Still alive.

She exhaled just as slowly. The second breath she took, however, was in reaction to the beauty surrounding her.

"It's gorgeous," she whispered. "I've never seen skies so crisp and blue."

"It's pretty amazing, isn't it?" Blake's voice had gone soft as well.

She glanced to the side and caught him looking at her. Her stomach tightened. Why had she ever thought his eyes were cold? Right now they were warm and alive, and looking at her like...

She shook herself. He was glad they'd broken through the clouds. Just like she was.

That shivery look he'd thrown her meant nothing more than that.

She leaned forward as several land masses came into view. Some of them stretched toward the sky like the volcanoes she knew them to be. "The Aleutians."

"Yes." The reverence behind the single word made her take

a closer look below. Her father had loved the islands, despite the treacherous conditions she constantly heard about in the news reports. She'd never understood why someone would willingly live in a place where fog, wind and icy conditions were almost constant companions.

Until now.

One of the distant island peaks wore a thick covering of clouds like a top hat. It brought a smile to her face.

"My father loved it here."

"I know." Blake's hands loosened on the wheel. "He told me."

Molly's mother had often complained he loved the islands more than his own family. Why else would he take a job most pilots chose to avoid? He could have had a nice cushy job as an airline pilot, and been better paid for his trouble. He'd turned a deaf ear to his wife's protests and as the years had gone by, her clinginess and grumbling had taken a toll on their relationship. If he hadn't been killed, Molly doubted their marriage would have survived another year.

It was one of the reasons she'd wanted to take the job, to try to see the islands through eyes that weren't tainted by bitterness.

The turbulence of the last half hour had made her rethink that decision. But the second they exited that storm, well, she'd been blown away.

The experience had been breathtaking. Magical.

She'd never seen anything like it in her life.

The plane banked slightly, heading toward the islands. She listened as Blake called in their position and requested permission to land.

As they descended, she craned her neck but couldn't see anything that looked like a landing strip. The mountains seemed to take up every inch of surface space. "Where's the airport? Is it on the other side of the island?"

"Nope, we're heading right for it."

All she saw was a short road bisecting a narrow pinch of land. The pavement went nowhere, both ends dumping into the…

Ocean.

"You're kidding me. That?" She wedged herself into her seat as Blake pushed the yoke farther in, increasing their rate of descent. *Oh, Lord.* "You've landed this before, right?"

"Many times. Relax."

Easy for him to say. If they set down too early or too late, they'd be swimming instead of flying.

Or worse.

As the plane continued to descend, the turbulence picked up again. Molly tried to remain calm, but ended up back in her original takeoff position, both hands gripping her seat, fervently praying she'd live to see another day.

Down, down, down they went. Just when she was sure the wheels were going to trail through the whitecaps below, the landing strip reached for them, grabbing them to safety.

Or so she thought.

Nothing could have prepared her for the bone-jarring conditions of the asphalt as they hurtled down the strip and toward what looked like the end of the world.

Her fingers tightened with each yard they gained, the brakes of the plane throwing her against her shoulder harness. She pressed down with both feet, hoping the plane would intuitively figure out that she wanted it to S-T-O-P. Now!

What seemed to take forever was, in all probability, over in a matter of seconds. They slowed to taxi speed, with several yards of runway to spare. Okay, so it was more than that, but when you were landing on something the size of a small driveway, any extra room between you and disaster was a welcome sight.

"Are you all right over there?" Blake turned the controls,

and they powered toward a building that stood at right angles to the landing strip.

"Yeah. Fine." She hoped he didn't notice the way her voice cracked from one word to the next.

"See? We made it all in one piece." He squeezed her wrist and, as if he'd pressed a switch, her hands released their hold of the seat. "You did great, by the way. The first time is always the hardest. But, believe me, once you get used to it, you'll find yourself wanting to do it every chance you get."

CHAPTER THREE

HAD he really just said that?

Blake jerked his hand from hers. Any hope that she'd missed his unfortunate choice of words flew out the window when color flared along her cheekbones.

Serve him right if she took off to find a new pilot, especially after the way he'd acted on the flight. He'd been angry when he'd realized how afraid she was of flying. Leave it to him to be attracted to women who were the worst possible match for someone like him. First Sharon and then Molly.

He'd always thought Sharon would come around, but she hadn't.

And now he'd unintentionally compared flying to sex with the next girl who came within range of his radar. Two for two. Yeah, he was in rare form.

Shutting off his internal critic, he went about his after-flight check. Molly unhooked her restraint harness and turned toward him.

"Thanks for getting us down in one piece. I know I probably haven't been your easiest passenger." She paused as if expecting him to heartily agree. "But I appreciate you not turning around and hauling my butt back to Anchorage."

"Would that have been before we entered the storm, or after we came out?"

She tried on a smile. "Just so you know I didn't set out to deceive you. I never claimed to be a seasoned traveler."

"I know. Your reaction on takeoff just took me by surprise. Sorry for being rude." He stood to unlock the door, then followed her down the steps as they exited the plane. Once they hit the tarmac, the ground crew met them, asking about their bags. He squared everything away then crossed to where she stood.

"I don't blame you for not wanting to fly with me again, but..." She paused as if gathering her thoughts. "I'd appreciate it if you'd give me a lift home tomorrow. I promise you won't have to sweet-talk me onto the plane."

Despite the sun shining down on them, super-chilled air quickly found its way into the collar and sleeves of his leather jacket. He could do without the constant wind on the islands. Or the reminder of how his marriage had crashed and burned. Against his better judgment, he asked, "You sure?"

"Sure you won't have to sweet-talk me?"

He shifted his weight, trying not to think about how he might like to do just that. "No, I meant are you sure you want *me* to fly you home? I was serious about hooking you up with an experienced pilot."

Glancing at his face, she bumped him with her shoulder and wrinkled her nose. "You've seen how I handle rough weather. Do you really want to foist that on some other unsuspecting soul?"

So she could laugh at herself. His shoulders lost some of their tension.

Actually, now that they were on the ground, she was charming and funny. "Well, since you put it that way, maybe it would be better for everyone if we stuck to our original arrangement. For this trip, anyway."

"My thoughts exactly." She wrapped the flapping ends of her jacket around herself and zipped it tight. The stiff breeze played with her hair, lifting the short strands up and away from her face, before allowing them to fall in delightful disarray. "Now, if you could point me in the direction of the nearest diner, I have two urgent needs."

"Food?"

"That's second on my list. The first is to find a heater that actually works. No offense, but my toes are still frozen from the flight." She pursed her lips. "But I *could* go for a nice hot meal, now that my stomach's starting to settle down. The cold is good for something, anyway."

"I know where they make a mean crab cake. I could show you around the island afterward." He shoved his hands into the pockets of his leather coat, trying to keep the cold from encroaching any further. It was evidently disrupting his thought processes. "You've seriously never been here before?"

"Nope. First time, remember?"

Just like that flight out. Hard to believe she'd lived in Alaska all her life and had never visited the islands.

Sharon had called Unalaska "quaint" on her first visit. Until she'd realized there was no mall. No fashion boutiques. Just simple, hard-working folks. She'd quickly felt trapped—had run back home before six months had been up. He'd do well to keep that in mind before he went and did something stupid.

Like offer to eat lunch with Molly and show her the sights? Who knew how long she'd even stick around?

She was terrified of flying. Her *mother* was afraid of flying. If she had a dog, a cat, or a chipmunk, it would probably be petrified as well. It didn't bode well for someone who'd be medevacing patients on a regular basis. Even as he told himself distance was his friend in a situation like this, he'd already committed himself as tour guide for a day.

Damn. No backing out now. But after lunch and a quick trip around the island, he'd put his pro-distance plan into motion.

Over a basket of crab cakes and fries, Molly grilled him about the islands. She already knew the obvious stuff, like the reality show dealing with the perils of deep-sea fishing that was filmed here, and that the island chain separated the Bering Sea from the Northern Pacific. But she seemed fascinated by some of the quirkier details. Dutch Harbor and Unalaska were essentially the same community separated by a short bridge, but the arguments about which name was correct continued unabated. Both names had stuck. Dutch Harbor was used for the port and business sections, while Unalaska was where everyone lived when the workday was through.

"So, if *Aleutians* comes from a native word for island, doesn't that make it redundant to call them the Aleutian *Islands*?"

He took a sip of his soda, then leaned back in his seat. "I guess it does."

"How long have you been flying this route?"

"Seven years, but I grew up here."

"And you said my father helped train you?"

Setting his drink back on the table, he nodded. "Yes. I already had my pilot's license, but decided I wanted something with a little more oomph."

"Like Evel Knievel. I remember." Her brows went up. "My mom never understood why my dad wanted to leave a relatively safe job as a commercial pilot in order to be a bush pilot."

He tensed, hoping she wasn't going to ask him if Wayne had talked about his family. Because, while Wayne had loved his wife and daughter, he'd given serious thought to ending his marriage and moving away. His mentor's misgivings had echoed his own. It had taken Blake two years from the time of Wayne's death to realize Sharon's attitude wasn't going to change. After forcing him to leave one job, she'd ended up hating its replacement just as much, more so once they'd moved to his old house on the islands.

The home where he'd been born and raised—given to him when his parents had retired and moved to Florida—had gone from a place of happy memories to a battle zone where no one had ever won. The happiness his parents had found with each other seemed to elude him. When Sharon had finally filed for divorce, he'd been secretly relieved.

"The weather's not always as bad as it was today." No. Not always. Sometimes it was much worse.

He motioned at her empty plate, ready to be done with this particular conversation. "If you're finished, I can show you where the clinics—the two that are currently functioning, anyway—and the hotel are. Are you staying at the Grand Aleutian?"

"No, I'm at the UniSea."

He'd expected her to spring for the pricier accommodations, although he wasn't sure why. Maybe because it was what Sharon would have done. "I have a house here, but I can drop you off at the hotel."

"If I take the job, I may end up renting something."

If I take the job.

Blake motioned for their check. "That flight didn't scare you off?"

"Maybe. We'll see. A lot of it depends on whether or not there are enough patients to make it a wise use of funds. Alaska Regional agreed to partner with the clinic for a year. After that…who knows? There's plenty of need in Anchorage, if not." Her lips tightened. "Or in one of the other big cities in the lower forty-eight."

Big cities. Was that a prerequisite?

When the waitress came with the bill, he waved off Molly's attempt to pay. "I'll turn it in for reimbursement. No sense in each of us filling out an expense report."

"Thanks. My turn next time."

Next time.

Right. Like that was ever going to happen. He needed to bow out of this gig as soon as possible.

But as she moved from the booth and stretched her slender frame, his resolve seemed to dry up—along with his mouth.

The heavy jacket she'd shrugged out of while they were eating had done a thorough job of hiding her figure, as did the white lab coat she normally wore in the ER. But the creamy white sweater had no such problem. Soft and clingy, it skimmed over each and every curve all the way to the middle of her thighs, where dark jeans bridged the gap between the sweater and her knee-high leather boots.

Hell, she was gorgeous.

Maybe he should rethink this.

Crazy. Allowing a flicker of attraction to dictate his actions could never end well.

They moved outside, and Blake clicked the lock on the car he'd left at the airport.

Molly hesitated before getting in. "I should have rented a car. I don't expect you to be my taxi service while I'm here."

"The island's not that big, so it's no trouble. Once I drop you off at the hotel, though, I'll need to head home and get some rest before the flight tomorrow. So if you're looking to take in some of the night life, you're on your own."

At least his mouth had finally got with the program.

The last thing he wanted was to see another woman's lip curl at what the island had to offer in that regard.

"I'm an early riser, actually, so I think I'll turn in after dinner." She tilted her head back to glance at him. "Besides, I want to make sure I don't miss my flight. The pilot didn't seem all that inclined to wait around."

Several strands of hair slid across her cheek as she looked at him, exposing a delicate earlobe. It took more effort than he expected not to reach out and sift his fingers through the shiny locks to see if they were as soft and silky as they looked.

"I'll be there." The temptation to touch her washed through him again. But before he could, she opened the car door and got inside.

He climbed in as well, irritated by the repeated tugs of attraction. Being trapped inside the closed vehicle just made the situation worse. He'd been too busy during their flight to notice the delicate mixture of vanilla and clean sea spray that clung to her skin. Now the scent drifted toward him, making its way inside his head.

Damn. Erasing that fragrance from his memory was going to be impossible. The image of sliding his nose along the naked length of her neck and inhaling deeply rose unbidden, and he gritted his teeth.

The sooner he dropped her off the better.

This whole trip carried a surreal element he struggled to understand. Some of the nurses at the hospital had thrown him looks that held veiled invitations, but he'd never been tempted to return the flirtation or even ask for a phone number. He valued his hard-won freedom far too much to risk messing things up. And he had no intention of moving back to Anchorage to be with another woman.

But his reaction to Molly made him wonder if he was really as immune to the opposite sex as he liked to think. He started the car and tried to put the thought out of his mind. Unfortunately the very thing he'd decided *not* to think about ended up being the one subject he couldn't banish.

Go home. Take a shower. Go to sleep.

If he could do those things, in that order, this whole crazy day would soon be behind him. Before he knew it, Molly McKinna would be out of his life forever. Unless she actually decided to stay on the island, in which case they were bound to run into each other on a regular basis. And there was the fact that he was one of the few medevac pilots who flew these islands. But that didn't mean he and Molly had to be anything more than casual acquaintances or professional colleagues. She would still be tied to the hospital in Anchorage and would probably return there eventually.

He gave himself a mental thump.

Thick skull, meet harsh reality. You two are about to become really good friends.

Molly stood in the white-tiled waiting room of the clinic as Blake made the introductions. Sammi Trenton, the community health aide, tossed her thick dark braid over her shoulder. Tall and slender with high cheekbones that spoke of an island heritage, the young woman smiled in welcome. CHAs played a huge role in healthcare in Alaska, especially in the Aleutians, where population density was low and funding dollars were scarce. Learning about the medical problems the island faced on a regular basis would give Molly a head start for when she actually came to work in a few weeks. Besides, she could do with a few friends right about now.

"Glad to have you." Sammi shook her hand. "We could sure use the help. Hope you plan on sticking around longer than…"

The woman's eyes cut to Blake, a playful smirk on her face. "Oops. Sorry. Don't know where that came from."

"Still kicking me in the shins after all these years, I see."

Sammi's brows lifted. "I didn't have a choice back then. That was the only thing I could reach." She glanced at Molly. "I was the runt who always got picked on."

"You were the runt who always did the picking on," Blake returned, with an easy smile that carved out a deep groove in his cheek.

Molly's heart rolled over for a second before righting itself. *Okay. No staring.* She forced her gaze back to Sammi.

"How was the flight in?" Sammi tilted her head at Blake, her thumb rubbing at a tiny spot on her monkey-stamped smock.

Great. Here it came. The perfect opportunity for Blake to get in a shot at Molly's expense. She tensed in preparation.

"We hit a stormy patch on the way in, but once we got through it, it was smooth sailing."

A sardonic brow lifted in her direction made her wonder if he was referring to the actual weather or to the clash of tempers that had gone on between them. As for *smooth sailing*, that was yet to be seen.

"Well, now that you're here, let me give you the grand tour. Besides, that'll give us girls a chance to get to know each other better."

Blake's brow furrowed. "Be nice."

"*Moi*? I'm always nice." She motioned for Molly to follow her through the door that led to the back of the clinic, wiggling her fingers at Blake as a goodbye.

Although these two were obviously friends from way back, nothing seemed to suggest there was anything more between them than that. Even if there was, it was none of her business. She had to admit, though, they'd make a gorgeous couple, with Blake's rugged good looks and Sammi's dark hair and striking features. And the other woman was tall enough to almost look Blake in the eye, whereas Molly barely reached his chin. Talk about runts.

Sammi took her to one of the exam rooms which, along with the familiar scent of disinfectant, was clean, airy and well appointed. The soft green walls and creamy Formica countertops gave the space a cool, calm atmosphere, a definite plus when working with worried parents or frightened youngsters. "We have three exam areas, but there's normally only one of us on duty at any given time. Having the Anchorage hospital sponsor you will make our jobs a lot easier."

"You said, 'our.' What's the staffing like?"

"We have two receptionists, a nurse and a PA, who can also write prescriptions. During medevacs, things get hectic because someone has to accompany the patient." She gave an innocent blink. "That's where you come in, right? You'll be taking over that part of the job, unless we have more than one emergency."

Molly was tempted to plead ignorance and say she was strictly part of the ground crew, but the hospital had specifically wanted one of their own doing the medical transports. So that line of reasoning wasn't going to fly. "That's what they tell me."

"Blake's great. You'll like working with him."

This was her chance. "You've known each other a long time?"

Sammi led her back out into the hallway and pushed open a door to the restroom, so Molly could see it. "We grew up together, so I guess you could say that." She hesitated. "His ex put him through the wringer a couple of years back. He can be a bit touchy about the subject."

"Understandable." Molly was a little raw from her own experience with her ex, Gary, so she'd be happy to swing clear of that particular subject.

The door at the end of the hallway opened to a tiny break room, complete with refrigerator and microwave. There was also a cot along one wall. "You spend the night?"

"Every once in a while, if we're waiting on a birth or need to transport a patient to the airport to be medevaced. But we all carry cellphones. If there's an emergency, most folks know how to reach us after hours. Are you okay with going on the phone list?"

"Of course. Anything I can do to help."

"Now for the all important question: when do you want to start?"

Molly swallowed. If she wanted to back out, now was the time. But Sammi was so nice, seemed eager for her to take some of the load off the other workers. And she really, *really* didn't want to go back to Anchorage and face Gary day in and day out or field his constant calls. He refused to believe it was really over, even after six months. As did her mother. Was it really fair to allow them both to keep holding out hope?

No. It wasn't. "I have to go back to Anchorage to finish packing. I could probably start in two weeks. Oh, and I'll need to find a place to rent. Do you know of anything?"

"Let me check and give you a call in the morning. Blake says you'll be over at the hotel? We'll find you something. Any preferences?"

"Not really. Just a place to sleep. Nothing fancy."

"Good, because nothing fancy is what Unalaska does best." She squeezed Molly's hand. "Just leave it to me. Now I'd better get you back to Blake before he has a hissy fit. See you in two weeks?"

"Definitely."

And if Blake didn't want to fly her back in two weeks, well, like he'd said, there were plenty of pilots where he came from.

Molly awoke to the sound of something pinging against the windowpane of her hotel room. Squinting, she tried to see the clock.

Too blurry.

Ugh, her contacts were still on the nightstand. She reached over and felt around for the glasses she'd left next to her contacts case. Slipping them on, she glanced again at the clock.

Her heart stalled in her chest.

Seven-thirty! She was supposed to be at the plane in a half hour.

Blake hadn't asked about her breakfast plans or mentioned

picking her up and taking her to the airport. In fact, by the time he'd shown her around the island and dropped her off at the hotel yesterday afternoon, he'd seemed all too anxious to be rid of her. He'd said goodbye with a wave of his hand, before getting back in his car and driving away to wherever he lived.

He'd probably been exhausted from their flight and from schlepping around with her all day. Molly loved the clinic, and Sammi had seemed especially nice, not a hint that she or anyone else viewed her as a threat.

Except maybe Blake, who'd said she needed to be strapped into her seat by eight o'clock.

Or else. Leaping out of bed, she scrambled for her clothes, thankful she'd taken a shower the previous night to banish the chill that had burrowed deep into her bones.

The pinging noise outside was still going strong, like someone throwing pebbles repeatedly against the glass. Well, she could think of at least one person she could rule out, if that was the case.

She tiptoed to the window, clothes in hand, and parted the curtains several inches. Still dark. Then she caught the glitter of stones on the sidewalk.

No, not stones. Hail. The size of gumballs.

And it wasn't just hailing. Now that she was awake, she realized the gloom was caused by heavy gray clouds that covered the sky. The wind was also howling, kicking up leaves and sending some of the scattered ice drops skittering down the walkway. Her fingers tightened around the clothing she held. Even if she made it to the airport on time, could they take off in these conditions?

Please, no. She'd already flown through one storm. The last thing she wanted to do was make a bigger fool out of herself than she had yesterday.

With her luck, no pilot in his right mind would agree to fly with her after that.

And by the end of the day Blake had seemed so...

Impatient.

He was probably dreading the return trip as much as she was. Maybe she'd be better off not even taking the job.

Except she'd promised Sammi she would, and the hospital was counting on her to follow through. And this job was a lifeline, appearing just when she'd really needed it.

Apart from the flying, which she wondered if she could do—especially while dealing with critically ill patients—she found she liked the island and its inhabitants. She knew the biggest industry was fishing, but was surprised to learn the port itself did quite a bit of business. As they'd driven around yesterday, Blake had pointed out a huge vessel stacked high with various-colored shipping containers getting ready to dock.

She continued to stare out the window, wondering what she should do, when a dark familiar shadow stopped in front of her door. With one hand shoved deep into his pocket, Blake braced himself against the wind, preparing to knock. Just as she got ready to slam the curtains back together, their eyes met.

Argh! Too late.

She still had on the sweatpants and threadbare white tank top she'd worn to bed. And if she could see him, he could see...

His lips quirked, and a rush of heat poured into her face. She held up a finger, hoping he'd catch her meaning. Maybe she could get dressed really fast and...

Poor guy. It was freezing out there. She glanced down. It wasn't like she was in a negligee or anything. She could at least let him into the room while she ducked into the bathroom to get dressed.

Padding over to the door, she made sure her clean clothes were draped to conceal key areas of her chest before opening it. "Come in. I'm running a little late—sorry."

"I tried to call, but they're having trouble with the phones evidently, because I couldn't get through." He glanced at her as if seeing her for the first time. "Uh, I can wait out here until you get ready."

"Don't be ridiculous. It's hailing. Besides, I'm freezing standing here."

That worked. He slid through the opening and let her shut the door behind him.

Heading for the bathroom, she called behind her, "I'll just be a minute."

Once she made it safely inside, she leaned against the wall. Did she even want to look in the mirror?

She opened her eyes and peered into the reflective surface.

Glasses. Great. They weren't even her good pair. And she'd left her contact case on the nightstand.

Leaning closer, she moaned at the sight that met her eyes. Tangled hair, sticking out every which way. Waistband of her sweatpants skewed way to one side, creating a series of un-flattering wrinkles that slanted from right to left. And was that a piece of sleep?

Yep. Right in the corner of her eye.

She dropped her head in her hands and moaned. Maybe if she stayed in the bathroom long enough, he'd go away and let her die in peace. He looked clean, rested and, most of all, well groomed.

He smelled good, too, like he'd just hopped out of the shower.

Well, all she could do was work with what she had. He'd just seen her at her worst, so even dragging her fingers through her hair would be an improvement.

She worked as fast as she could, dressing in jeans and a

heavy turtleneck, scrubbing her teeth and face then sweeping a coat of clear gloss over her lips. Once she'd finished, there was a moment or two when she entertained the thought of hiding out for a while, before deciding to be a big girl and face him. One deep breath later, she'd opened the door.

Camped out in a chair, Blake sat next to the bed, which was a wreck from all the tossing and turning she'd done during the night. His elbows were propped on his knees as he stared at the images flickering across the weather channel. He glanced up, his eyes sweeping over her as she came into the room. He sat up straighter.

"I like your…er, glasses. I didn't notice them yesterday."

"That's because I wore contacts." That he'd had to scrounge around for something nice to say couldn't be good. She gave an internal shrug. So what if she'd noticed every incredible inch of him from the moment he'd climbed aboard that plane, while he barely even remembered what she looked like?

She squared her shoulders. The last thing she was trying to do was impress him. "How's it looking out there?"

"Not good. I think we might end up staying another—"

A knock at the door interrupted whatever he'd been about to say. Molly frowned at him in question before hurrying over to fling it open.

"Dr. McKinna?" A man, shrouded in a drab green raincoat, stood in the doorway, his head covered by the jacket's hood. Even shadowed, and with water sluicing down his face, she thought she saw worry in his eyes.

"Yes. Is something wrong?"

"Sammi said she tried to reach you by phone and couldn't get through, so she asked me to drive over and see if you were still here. There's a man down over at the dockyard." He braced himself against a gust of wind, and Molly had to hold the door to prevent it from being ripped from her hands.

Blake came up behind her, the heat from his body warming her back.

"Hi, Mark," he said, confirming his presence. "What's going on?"

"The damn wind knocked a container sideways and it caught one of the workers in the leg. I was checking on a shipment for a customer and saw it happen. It's bad, there's bone showing through. I came to see if the doc here could take a look." He glanced at her just as a growl of thunder rumbled through the atmosphere, bringing with it another blast of wind. Her fingers scrabbled to retain their hold of the door just as the man's next words chilled her to the bone. "If there's any way you can get the plane up, he needs to be transported out. The sooner, the better."

CHAPTER FOUR

"HAVE you moved him?"

Yanking on her jacket, Molly's mind ran through various scenarios. Compound fractures could be tricky. When a bone ripped through skin and muscle and was left open to the elements, infection could easily follow. The less sanitary the accident location, the worse it was for the patient, especially if anything outside the body had contaminated the exposed bone.

The man who Blake called Mark dragged a hand through his hair. "No, the bone is… Hell, it looked so bad, no one dared. The men threw a couple blankets over him and were rigging some plastic to keep him dry until I could find you. I'd medevac him myself, but Blake's plane is basically a flying ambulance. Mine just doesn't have that kind of equipment."

"You made the right decision." Although she hated to think of an injured man out in this weather, she didn't want that exposed bone receiving additional damage from attempts to drag him to another site. And she hoped to God those blankets were clean. "How much bleeding is there?"

"Some. But nothing's gushing."

Thank God. No severed arteries.

"Is he conscious?"

Mark shook his head. "As soon as he hit the ground, he was out cold."

Blake had gone out to warm up the car without being asked, for which she was grateful.

She and Mark hurried outside, and Molly slammed the hotel room door behind them. "We'll follow you, okay?"

"You bet. The crate fell across the aisle, so we'll have to circle around a bit to reach him, but at least it'll block the worst of the wind."

After she jumped into the car, Blake accelerated, following the taillights in front of them. "Put your hands over the vent. It'll help keep them warm until we get there."

She yanked off her gloves and held them over the heated flow of air. Not because it felt good, but because the warmer her hands stayed now, the more nimble they would be once they arrived. For a pilot, Blake knew a thing or two about medicine. But then again he flew rescue missions all the time. It gave her another insight into her father. By the time of his death he must have known almost as much as the EMTs and nurses he'd worked with.

"How far to the dockyard?" she asked.

"With the weather, fifteen minutes or so. It's in Dutch Harbor, so we won't have to cross the bridge into Unalaska." He clicked the wipers into high gear to keep up with the sleety rain as they followed Mark's taillights.

She peered into the sky. Heavy gray clouds. No sign of the rain letting up any time soon. "Why would anyone work in weather like this?"

"Sometimes you don't have a choice." He slid a glance at her, his lips tight. "*You're* working."

"Yes, but this is an emergency. And it's my job."

"Mine, too. The dockyard folks have to work as well, even if it's just to secure the area."

He had a point. And in a place famous for its rough weather, it probably came down to working or going hungry.

This was what her father must have faced time and time again. And yet he'd claimed to love it.

Why?

By the time they got to the container area, her thoughts had shifted to the job at hand. Blake followed Mark as he cruised between aisles of stacked containers.

So big.

She swallowed. "Can you imagine if one of these fell on somebody?"

"Yeah. I can."

He'd not only imagined it, he'd seen it up close, if his tense jaw was anything to go by.

"Did he live?"

"Who?"

"The person you're thinking about."

A quick shake of his head conveyed his meaning all too well. Crush injuries were among the worst. And if the crate landed directly on top of someone…

The truck in front of them pulled to a stop, and Molly immediately spied a huge blue tarp stretched between two shipping containers.

She pulled the hood of her coat into place since it was still sleeting, grabbed her medical bag, then exited the vehicle. She was vaguely aware that Blake had also gotten out. Hurrying around Mark's parked car, she found four men standing under the plastic, with a fifth man kneeling next to the victim, who appeared to be unconscious at the moment. The patient's pale face and the slightly blue cast to his lips signaled shock. Her eyes quickly scanned the body through the blanket.

Crouching next to him, she felt for a pulse—which seemed strong enough—before pulling back the layers of blankets from his bottom half, noting the fabric of his work pants had been slit up the middle, laying bare his leg from ankle to groin. Good thinking.

The fracture was in the left femur, the jagged edge of the exposed bone pointing to the left as if thumbing a lift out of there.

Soon. I promise.

The other half of the break was nowhere to be seen, hidden somewhere deep inside his leg. But if it looked anything like the bone she *could* see… Her stomach knotted. Move him the wrong way and the sharp edges could indeed slice through an artery and kill him.

"How long's he been unconscious?"

One of the men behind her answered. "About a half hour, maybe a little longer. I saw the whole thing. He was out as soon as his head hit the ground."

"How hard did he hit?" She made a mental note to check for signs of a concussion or skull fracture.

"Pretty hard. And once we saw the angle of the leg, we knew it was broken. We just cut his pant leg to see how bad it was." The man swallowed hard. They hadn't expected to find what they had.

She slipped on a pair of latex gloves then used her thumb to pull back the wounded man's right eyelid. Flicking the beam from her penlight across the pupil, she then repeated the action with the other eye.

Equal and reactive. Good. No evidence of brain trauma at the moment.

Working quickly, she again took his pulse, then ran her hands down his unaffected limbs, making sure she wasn't missing another obvious fracture. Everything felt solid.

Blake knelt beside her. "What can I do?"

"I want to get an IV into him, but we can do that once we get to the plane. Right now, I need to stabilize his leg. Can you find me some heavy sticks or a couple pieces of lumber? Not too long, maybe—"

She held her hands apart, approximating the size she wanted.

"I'm on it."

He hadn't balked at the task, neither had he batted an eyelash at the sight of the man's open wound. Evel Knievel or not, he was evidently good at his job.

While he was gone, she grabbed a small bottle of saline and sponged away the blood so she could see the area better. She then wet several pieces of sterile gauze and laid them over the wound, one on top of the other, to keep the bone moist and avoid further contamination. Those layers were topped with a few dry ones, in case the bleeding continued. Blake was back by the time she was done, holding a couple of clean-looking one-by-fours.

"These okay?"

"Perfect." She nodded toward her bag. "I've got some hand sanitizer and some surgical gloves in there. I'll need you to help me splint him, if you're up to it."

As soon as she said it, she glanced up to make sure he was in agreement, but he'd already handed off the wood to someone else and was squirting the sanitizer onto his hands.

"Does anyone have a truck or a van we can use to transport him to the airport? Something with a large covered area?"

Neither of the local clinics were equipped to do surgery like this, and Anchorage had a great orthopedic surgeon who was willing to come in at a moment's notice. She'd radio it in once they were in the air.

"I do." The man who'd been kneeling next to the patient spoke up. "It's in the parking lot."

She noticed his hesitation and wondered if he was worried about liability issues. "I'll take responsibility," she said.

"It's not that. He's going to be okay, isn't he? He's…he's my…"

When the man's voice cracked, Mark spoke up. "They're

brothers. Jed—your patient—lost his wife to cancer a few months ago. He's got two young kids at home."

Oh, boy.

She turned to the man who couldn't have been older than his early twenties. No need for him to see what she was about to do. "We're going to take good care of him, I promise. Do you think you could bring your truck as close as you can? Once we splint his leg, we'll be ready to go."

"Sure." He glanced one last time at his brother as keys exchanged hands, then got to his feet and strode away.

"Do we need to contact someone?" she asked Mark.

"I'll call his sister. She can watch the kids when they get out of school." He took a step closer, his eyes narrowing in on hers. "Listen, I appreciate you coming down here with me."

"Hey, it's what I'm here for. No need to thank me."

He smiled, his mouth opening as if to say something else, when a sharp snap sounded next to her yanking her attention back to Blake, who rubbed the area where his surgical glove met bare skin. A glimmer of irritation shone in his blue eyes.

At what? They weren't even in the air yet.

She gave a mental shrug. Men!

"I'm going to have you hold the wood on either side of his leg, from upper thigh down to midcalf. I'll wrap gauze around the whole thing to immobilize it." She raised her brows. "You sure you're going to be okay?"

"I usually am."

The annoyance she'd thought she'd seen in his eyes was in his voice as well.

What the hell was wrong with him?

Without another word she positioned the pieces of wood and motioned for Blake to hold them in place. She then made a coil of about twenty loops of gauze, so she wouldn't have to repeatedly lift his leg, then slid Jed's foot carefully through the center of the bundle, easing it past his knee until it was draped around the makeshift splint. Separating the loops, she positioned them, making sure the moist pieces of gauze she'd placed a few minutes ago were still covering the wound and that the bone hadn't shifted. Satisfied, she tugged the slack out of the bindings, her stomach tightening when the man suddenly groaned and shifted on the ground, his eyes rolling back in his head.

Please don't regain consciousness. Not yet.

The pain would be agonizing if he woke up before she finished. She tied the upper portion of the bandage so it wouldn't unravel. She repeated the process on the bottom half of his leg, working as fast as she could. He didn't cry out again, however, and she breathed a sigh of relief when she fastened the last knot.

"Can you give him some morphine?" A sheen of moisture had appeared on Blake's upper lip, despite the cold. He wasn't as unaffected as he seemed.

"Not until we get to the plane. I don't want to risk it without having an IV hooked up."

The sound of wheels crunching on loose gravel signaled the vehicle's arrival. She eyed a nearby piece of plywood. "I want to use that as a back brace. I'll need three men to stabilize his neck and back and to turn him while I slide that wood underneath him. Volunteers?"

Mark immediately moved to her left side, two others kneeling next to him. "Tell us what to do."

Beside her, Blake stiffened before climbing to his feet and stripping off his gloves. "I'll get the wood."

"Thanks."

On her signal, they rolled Jed onto his side, while she and Blake maneuvered the plywood into place. "Okay, lay him back, gently."

Blake and the men carried the injured man to the truck and slid him inside. Freezing rain pelted her once again as she ducked from beneath the plastic tarp and climbed into the back of the vehicle. She had to bend over at an awkward angle to keep from hitting the roof of the pick-up shell. Away from the shelter of the fallen shipping crate, the wind caught the truck, jostling it back and forth.

Another long and terrible flight to look forward to. Great.

Leaning down to peer inside the truck, Mark reached in and squeezed her hand for a long moment, before releasing it to pull a card out of his wallet. He handed it to her. "If you ever need a charter pilot, I'm available."

Wow, this place was just brimming with flyboys. What was it with this island?

"Thanks." Good to know, if Blake kept his word and abandoned her.

Mark hesitated, and a thread of irritation ran through her. They needed to get a move on. Before she could voice the words, he said, "Can you call and let me know how Jed's doing once you get to Anchorage?"

"Sure thing." She glanced around for Blake, who stood off to the right, arms folded across his chest, water streaming down his face. When Mark took a step back and nodded at him, he didn't move a muscle. He could have been made out of stone. Motioning him over, she asked, "Can you drive ahead and get the back of the plane set up for us?"

One brow went up as he glanced at the card in her hand.

She had no idea what she'd done, but this was ridiculous. Shoving Mark's card into the pocket of her jacket, she stared right back at him. If he had something to say to her, he could do it right now.

Instead, he turned and stalked toward his car, shoulders stiff, moving through the punishing rain and wind as if it were a spring shower. She watched him until he was out of sight. "Okay, Mark. Tell Jed's brother to head for the airport."

The ride there was almost as rough as the flight to Dutch

Harbor had been. She braced her back against the side of the truck to maintain her balance. She also had to anchor her patient the best she could to keep his pallet from scooting from one side of the truck bed to the other—no easy feat, since the man probably weighed close to two hundred twenty pounds—most of which was solidly packed muscle.

She really needed to work out more.

The vehicle slowed to a stop, and before she had time to wonder whether they'd just stopped at a red light or reached their destination, the glass at the back of the topper opened, and Blake peered in. "Everyone okay?"

He'd made an ass of himself back at the dockyard, but he'd seen that look in Mark's eye often enough to know what it meant. His buddy had seen something he liked—Molly—and he was about to take aim with his thousand-watt charm. He'd seen that stuff work on one too many women.

He and Mark had been friends since elementary school. They'd both grown up in Unalaska—had both graduated from high school together. And both had served in the military as pilots before Blake had turned to civilian pursuits. While he knew Mark had endured some hard knocks since leaving the service, that was no excuse for going through women like squares of cheese on a gourmet sampler tray.

Although, to be fair, it had never really bothered Blake. Before now.

Molly slid from the back of the truck, again pulling her hood over her head to protect herself from the rain. The soft, furry edge framed her face and brought her deep green eyes into sharp focus. "I should have asked Mark to come and help us load our patient. He's heavy. Even for you two guys." Jed's brother had joined them at the back of the truck.

Mark? Not a chance. Not even if Blake had to drag the patient, travois-style, across the tarmac all by himself. *Where had that come from?* If he were smart, he'd tell Molly to call the number on that business card and let his buddy ferry her back and forth across the ocean.

Why was he even hesitating when it was the perfect solution for everyone? Molly would get the handholding she evidently needed during flights, and he could put the memories of his ruined marriage out of his mind. The only time they'd ever have to deal with each other would be during medevacs, like this one. "I've got a wheeled stretcher on the plane. We'll use that."

Between the three of them they got the man into the back of the plane without letting him get soaked in the process. He still hadn't regained consciousness, though. Molly turned to the patient's brother. "I'd ask you to come along, but there's nothing you can do. Maybe you can make sure Jed's kids are taken care of. I'll call as soon as I know something." She fished a card out of her pocket—Mark's—and turned it over. "If you'll give me a number where I can reach you—"

"Sure, sure. It's…" He scrubbed his palm across his jaw as if struggling to remember what it was, then he appeared to get a grip, reciting the digits.

Molly scribbled it down. "Got it." She glanced up. "I promise I'll call as soon as we arrive."

"Thanks. I appreciate everything you've done, Doc."

"My pleasure. Take care."

Blake waved goodbye and climbed into the cargo area beside her, closing the door.

"What are you doing?"

"I thought you could use an extra pair of hands." The fact that the man still hadn't woken up worried him, especially with the weather conditions the way they were. According to the weather channel, it was going to stay this way until late this afternoon. He figured he could at least see if he could take some of the load off Molly's shoulders. Although why she'd wanted to come to the plane rather than ride out the weather at one of the clinics was beyond him.

Her brows came together as she worked to set up an IV. "Don't you have a plane to fly?"

The question hit him right between the eyes, and he suddenly realized why she'd chosen to head for the plane.

She thought he was going to take off in this weather? He'd have thought she, of all people, would be happy sitting on the ground for the next couple of hours. If she thought their trip to Dutch Harbor had been bad… "Have you looked at the sky recently?"

"Of course I have. But we need to get him to a hospital remember? The sooner the better." She'd repeated Mark's earlier words almost verbatim. Reaching out for the card she'd tossed onto a nearby table, she glanced down at it. As subtle a threat as he'd ever seen: if he wouldn't take her, she knew someone who would.

Anger churned through him. So she was suddenly the Fearless Flyer? No way. He was not about to be bullied into anything. Not by her. Not by Mark. Especially not into something that could get them all killed.

"I hate to disappoint you, Doctor. But you might want to take advantage of my help while you can. Because until this weather clears, we aren't going anywhere." He paused, then decided to drive his meaning home. "*No one* is."

CHAPTER FIVE

BLAKE was right.

The skies had magically cleared later that morning, allowing them to finally get off the ground. And the return flight had been a whole lot better sitting in the back with her patient, rather than up front where she could see how short that runway actually was as they careened toward the end.

She checked her watch. They'd been in the air for almost two hours. Her patient had come to soon after they'd got airborne, for which she was relieved. Not only did it keep her from dwelling on where she was—no easy feat—but she could assess his condition a little better as well. He was stable, the pulses in his injured leg strong and steady. No compartmental syndrome setting in. And she'd finally been able to give him a little pain medication to make him more comfortable.

"My kids?" He'd already asked that question a couple of times, making her heart ache.

"Mark promised to check with your sister, but I'll ask Blake if he's been able to speak with anyone. I'm sure they're fine."

Giving his shoulder a quick squeeze, she made her way to the front of the plane, holding on to one of the seats as she went. She'd ask him to check with the hospital while she was at it and make sure the orthopedic surgeon was standing by. At least it had been a relatively smooth flight so far, although by facing forward she could now see nothing but the air in front of them. Her stomach kicked up a protest as it had the two previous times she'd gone forward to ask Blake something.

She stood behind him and leaned close so he could hear her. "Hey. Everything okay?"

"Fine." Tension radiated off him as he threw a quick glance over his shoulder then faced forward again. "Jed hanging in there?"

"Yes, but he's asking about his kids again. Any luck raising his brother or Mark?" Molly tried to ignore the clean masculine scent coming off him. Tried to ignore the urge to scrape her cheek along the tiny grains of stubble that lined his firm jaw.

Knock it off, Moll.

"I reached his brother a few minutes ago. The kids will stay with him for the night. His sister's there as well. They're fine."

"Oh, good. I'll tell him." She turned to go back to her patient, but Blake stopped her.

"Molly?"

"Yes."

He hesitated. "You did a hell of a job back at the dockyard."

She blinked. "Uh, thanks. Working beats sitting up here worrying about how high we are."

"Feeling any better this time around?" The words were light enough, but there was an edge to them that put her on alert. Was he still mad?

"Anything's better than that storm we came through yesterday." If she wanted to apologize, now was the time to do it. "Sorry about demanding we take off. You were obviously right. I was just worried about Jed reaching the hospital quickly."

"It's okay." He glanced back again and his shoulders relaxed a bit. "Just for the record, I would have taken off if I was sure I'd make it. Evel Knievel and all."

She shivered. That's right. He'd have probably relished the challenge if she and Jed hadn't been on board.

And what happened to those he left behind, if it all went bad?

She shook off the morbid thought. "Well, anyway, he's doing fine."

When she turned around to head back, a hand on her wrist stopped her. His skin was warm against hers. "Can you sit for a minute?"

"I—I guess so. Just for a minute."

What was this all about?

Perching on the seat, she turned her body to face him. He scrubbed his knuckles along his jaw line in the exact spot she'd imagined sliding her cheek. A wave of heat swept over her. Focusing on the steady chill in the cockpit had no effect whatsoever.

She waited for him to say something, but when he remained silent, she spoke up. "Did you want to talk to me?"

He nodded. "About Mark. Well, he… What I mean is that…" His voice trailed away as the hand worrying the edge of his face moved to the back of his neck, the palm kneading the muscles.

"What about him?" Her heart dropped. "Is there something wrong with Jed's children after all?"

"No, no. Nothing like that." Again he stopped. "Mark is kind of a…"

What on earth was he trying to say?

"Kind of a what?"

"A ladies' man. He gets around."

She frowned. "And I need to know this because…?"

"Well, because…" one shoulder gave a quick shrug "…I think he might be interested in asking you out. Just wanted you to know he doesn't tend to stick around for the long haul."

She didn't know if she should be pleased or angry that Blake had taken it on himself to warn her off someone she barely knew. "And what gave you the idea he might ask me out?"

"He asked if I thought you'd say yes."

"I see." Except she didn't. Not at all. "And what did you tell him?"

Another shrug. "That he'd have to ask you himself."

She let that roll around her head for a few seconds. "Do you think he will?"

Molly hadn't even decided to take the job yet. The last thing she needed to be thinking about was getting involved with someone on the islands. Although, if Mark liked to keep things light with no commitments, getting too involved shouldn't be an issue. In fact, that kind of arrangement might even be ideal for someone like her. She'd never have to worry about disappointing him—he'd never start demanding more and more of her. And if Gary heard she was going out with someone else… Her brain grabbed onto that thought.

"He might. Which is why I decided to say something. We're friends and all, but I'd hate you to get the wrong idea about him."

The wrong idea. As if she couldn't figure things out on her own. Or as if she received so few offers from men that she'd be in danger of dragging him to the nearest jewelry store to shop for rings. After Gary? Not likely!

"Well, thanks for your concern, but I think I can take care of myself." She stood. "Speaking of which, I have someone else I should be caring for right now, so if you'll excuse me…"

"Sure."

He didn't even give her a sideways look as she headed toward the back.

Huh! Poor little Molly can't tell the difference between casual interest and a proposal of marriage. So we'll just explain how these things work.

Ooooh!

If he really *were* Evel Knievel, she wouldn't mind dumping him over the side of Snake River Canyon right now and daring him to make it to the other side. The nerve of the man!

Somewhere inside her, a little voice whispered that it wasn't Mark she should be worried about but—

Shut up.

Wiping his words from her mind, she knelt by her patient and dabbed a few beads of sweat from his brow with a dry cloth. The chill in the plane was numbing, yet Jed was dotted with perspiration. She'd given him a low dose of pain meds, but she didn't dare let him have any more. Not until they reached the hospital. Although his pupils still seemed fine, that crack on the head worried her a bit. He had quite a lump on the back of his skull. She'd probably order an MRI just to be safe.

His eyes opened. "Kids?"

"They're fine. They will be staying with your brother tonight. Mark's going to fly them all to Anchorage tomorrow, if you're still in the hospital."

Which he would be.

He sucked down a deep breath. "Good." He touched her arm. "Thanks."

Whereas the warmth of Blake's fingers had raised alarming little frissons of awareness along her skin, Jed's touch did absolutely nothing. All she felt was the invasive cold of the plane.

He's your patient. *You're not supposed to be attracted to him!*

She got up and plopped into a nearby seat, settling in for the rest of the flight.

One thing was certain, however. Flying had now become the least of her worries.

He wasn't looking for her.

Right. That's why he'd offered to give Mark, along with Jed's two kids, a lift from the airport this morning. Jed had been whisked away almost as soon as they'd arrived at the airport yesterday afternoon. Since the hospital had a length of runway almost butting up to one of its entrances, Molly, still holding the IV bag, had accompanied the stretcher from the plane to the double doors. A quick "Thanks" was all he'd got before they'd disappeared into the hospital.

What did you expect? You were her ride. Nothing else.

But that didn't stop his eyes from scouring every inch of the emergency room, wondering if she was working today.

Mark had charge of Jed's daughters so, when the girls were ushered in to see their father, Mark went with them. Where, even now, Molly was probably leaning against a nearby wall, tucking strands of her short dark hair behind her ears as she talked to him. Smiled at him.

Accepted his offer of dinner and a movie.

As she had every right to do.

From what he'd heard, the surgery on Jed's leg had been a success. He'd remain on heavy doses of IV antibiotics for the next day or so to make sure no infection took hold.

And Blake, smart guy that he was, had raised his hand and offered to take them all back to Dutch Harbor as soon as Jed was released from care, which meant he'd have to stick around Anchorage—his least favorite place—for a day or so, if he didn't get any other emergency calls. Yay, him.

He huffed out a breath. Well, he might as well pick up

some supplies while he was here. He'd call Sammi and see if the clinic needed anything.

He also needed to get a hold of Molly as he still had her suitcase in his car. Mark had gone to the hotel room and packed all her stuff—Blake's gut tightened at that thought—since neither he nor Molly had given a thought to her belongings in their mad dash to the dockyard. The knot of resentment grew even more, which was ridiculous. His friend had done nothing wrong.

Yeah, but I saw her first.

One hand tightened into a fist. What the hell was he, a little kid?

Funny how all that worry about flying with Molly—about how she'd react to the island once she saw it—hadn't stomped out the instant attraction he'd felt for her. In fact, her insistence on going up in that storm had been damned sexy. He'd seen a little bit of himself in her in that moment.

And now Mark was probably back there with her.

He dragged a hand through his hair and swore under his breath. He didn't even know if Molly was at the hospital.

Enough was enough.

Stepping outside, he made his way to the concrete "Emergency Room" sign a few yards away and leaned his elbows on it while he punched in a number on his cellphone.

"Hello?"

"Hey, Tony, Blake here." His boss ever since Wayne had died, Tony was as easygoing as they came.

"You back already? I thought you flew that new doctor to the islands."

"Yep, an emergency came up, and we had to come back in."

"What did she think?"

"I have no idea." He hesitated. If he was going to do this, he'd better do it now. Otherwise he was going to chicken out like a dumbass. He knew they'd have to fly together during medevacs, but she'd be in the back while he rode up front. Better to keep it to that as much as possible. "She's supposed to head back there in about two weeks. Any chance you can find another pilot to take her? How about Ronny?"

Silence reigned for half a minute. "Ronny? What gives? You asked for this gig in the first place. Is she that hard to work with?"

"No, it's just…" He forced the words out. "I think she'd do better with another pilot for the return trip. That's all."

Tony paused again. "You sure?"

"Yep, I am." Saying the words out loud might just trick his brain into believing them.

"Okay. I'll let you know what Ronny says. If he says no, you're stuck picking her up."

He wouldn't. Ronny never turned down the chance to fly. "Thanks. I owe you."

He clicked the phone shut, wishing he could walk away right now and never look back. But he had Mark and the kids to shuttle to a hotel, and then he'd have to fly everyone back to Unalaska while Mark's plane was being serviced here in Anchorage.

He'd be flying everyone except Molly.

And that's the way it was going to stay.

Before he could move away from the sign, she appeared out of nowhere. "Hey, there. I thought I saw you a few minutes ago. I was afraid I'd missed you."

"I'm giving Jed's kids and Mark a ride back to the hotel." He straightened, leaning his hip against the sign as he faced her. "How's Jed doing, by the way?"

"He's good. The surgeon had to put a pin in his femur. He'll be out of commission for a couple of months, but he should make a complete recovery." She smiled up at him. "Good thing you were part of his medical team, because these

HIPPA laws mean I have to…" She made a zipping motion across her mouth that made him smile.

Something in his chest gave a weird *ka-thunk* at her including him as part of the team, no matter what the reason. Maybe he should let her know he was no longer a part of it.

As soon as he figured out how.

"I appreciate the update, in any event. I bet his girls were glad to see him."

She laughed. "They're quite…active. But you should have seen Jed's face light up when they appeared in his doorway and tried to swarm his bed. It was really nice of Mark to take on flying them here, since Jed's brother had to work. Not many men would be up to the task."

The *ka-thunk* became a rock that dropped right to the pit of his stomach. "Yeah, he's a real…" *Tool. Nope. Wrong word. Try again.* "He's good with kids."

He cleared his throat, wanting to change the subject. "I meant to let you know that I've got your suitcase in my car. From the hotel?"

"Ah, yes. Thanks." Her fingers came up and flicked her hair behind her left ear—much as he'd imagined her doing earlier—revealing a delicate, perfect ear, which sported a simple pink bauble at the lobe.

The effect it had on him was exactly as he'd feared. He hardened instantly. Forcing himself to look away into the parking lot, he tried to take charge of his body. In the process, he spied a man and a very pregnant woman making their way toward the entrance. They stopped halfway to the door, and she pulled in a deep breath, blowing it out slowly, her cheeks puffing as she did. She was in labor—her husband supporting her as she breathed.

Lucky man. He'd have given anything to be the guy in that picture. To have the happy marriage his parents still shared.

But he didn't, and the possibility of that changing any time soon was slim to none.

His jaw hardened. "I'm just out in the lot. Where are you parked? Maybe we could transfer the case now."

"Sounds good. I'm just getting off duty. How about if I bring my car around, and I'll meet you out there?"

"I'll be standing about halfway down that third row."

"Great."

Blake tried not to notice the slight swing of her hips as she walked away with easy grace, but it was impossible. She was a beautiful woman. Confident. Kind.

And about to exit his life forever.

He headed toward his rental car, reaching in his pocket for the key. By the time he got her bag out of the car, she'd pulled up beside him. Climbing out of her car, she pushed a button on her keyring, unlocking the trunk of the compact. "I'll just throw it in the back. How did you manage to...?"

"Mark cleared out the room."

"Ah, that makes sense. Remind me to thank him."

He wouldn't be around to remind her of anything. If ever he was going to tell her about her new pilot, now was the time. He lifted the bag and put it into her trunk, rehearsing the sentence in his head. "Listen, about your next flight—"

"Hey, you two! I wondered where you went." Mark came up beside Molly, a little girl's hand in each of his own. He grinned at Blake, causing every muscle in his body to tighten. He recognized his friend's Cheshire-cat smile.

Mark was on the prowl, and he evidently wasn't above using Jed's two daughters to bait his trap.

"Did you get a chance to meet Jed's kids, Molly?"

"I did." She knelt down. "Hi, girls. Did you have a good visit with Daddy?"

"Yeah!" the one on the right said. "And Uncle Mark promised us ice cream on the way to the hotel."

"Lucky you." Molly kissed each of them on the cheek.

"Care to join us?" Mark's invitation grated across his last nerve, causing his hands to tighten.

"I wish I could, but my mother's expecting me." She sighed. "And I need to start packing."

"I guess we'll be seeing a lot more of you once you move to the island."

"I guess you will."

Well, he wasn't wasting much time! Nothing like having to stand there and watch the scene unfold in slow motion.

Molly gave the two girls another quick squeeze. "I'll see you both tomorrow at the hospital?"

Mark's smile widened. "I'll be there as well."

Climbing to her feet, she smiled back at him. There was silence for a couple of seconds, but before Blake could put a boot to the seat of Mark's jeans, his friend seemed to snap out of it.

"Well, it's getting late, and I need to get the girls to the hotel." He glanced at Blake. "You ready, old man?"

Since Blake was Mark's transportation, he didn't have much choice but to play along. So much for explaining to Molly about the change in plans.

Then again, it got him off the hook. She'd find out soon enough when she arrived at the airport and found another pilot waiting for her. It might be the coward's way out. But at this point that's exactly what he was.

A coward.

CHAPTER SIX

"WHY are you still in Unalaska? You're due back in Anchorage ASAP. Command performance—compliments of the top brass."

What the hell?

Blake sat up in bed, gripping his phone with one hand while fumbling to turn his clock to face him with the other.

Seven o'clock on Sunday morning—it was his first day off in ages, for crying out loud. "Is there an emergency?"

"You might say that. Seems your doctor friend is raising quite a stink about the pilot switch trick you played on her. She's having none of it. It's either you or she's out the door as far as the Unalaska job goes. And the hospital isn't any too happy about the prospect of those government dollars landing somewhere else, if she backs out."

"Slow down there, Tony. I have no idea what you're talking about."

"You're being tapped as Molly McKinna's official escort tomorrow morning. She's moving out to the island, right on schedule. I'm told that refusing is not an option at this point."

"You've got to be kidding me!" Anger shot up his spine as the last remnants of sleep deserted him. "What about Ronny?"

"Ronny's a tourist pilot. You and the doc will be working together on medevacs, so the bigwigs think you need to be more of a team player."

"Since when have they ever worried about that?"

His boss chuckled. "Since the doc got wind of the change in plans."

"What?"

"Someone told her you'd rather not take her, and she evidently took it personally." A sigh came over the line. "Maybe she's right, Blake. I don't know what happened between you two, but you're going to have to work together, so you might as well get used to it."

Really? He'd just got used to the idea of seeing her as little as possible. His skyrocketing heart rate told him he'd been right to draw a firm line in the sand and stay on the professional side of it. Hell, if he believed that being with someone like her wouldn't pop all the rivets he'd used to patch up his sorry life he'd have flown her without a qualm. Seven days a week, if that was what it took. But one last shred of sanity had stepped in and demanded to be heard. Besides, if Mark was interested...

Well, his friend was everything he wasn't.

Hell!

He kicked his way out from under the covers, half stumbling over them as he got out of bed. Hopping on one foot to regain his balance, he cursed under his breath and headed for the bathroom. What a way to start the day. "Okay, I'll meet her at the airport in the morning."

"Don't screw this up, Blake. That clinic needs her. You piss her off, and your job could be on the line."

"Yeah, well good luck finding someone to take my place."

The last thing Blake wanted was to get to the airport and hear about some date she and Mark had gone out on—without kids this time. Or fly through another storm with her. *Or* hear she'd decided she didn't like island life after all.

He hardly knew Molly, so why was he letting her get to him?

Because she was Wayne McKinna's daughter?

Maybe. But seeing her standing in the window of that hotel room, hair all mussed from sleep, a picture had formed in his head. Sleepy eyes blinking up at him. A whispered plea to come back to bed. Her soft, warm body welcoming his home.

The mental image had lit a fire within his chest that still burned.

Impossible. He'd barely got his life back on track. Which meant he had to face the possibility that Mark—and not him—might be the one who lived out that fantasy. A scenario he didn't want to watch unfold. Switching pilots was the best option. For everyone.

He gritted his teeth.

The silence on the other end of the phone line made him realize Tony had said something and was waiting for a reply. "I didn't catch that."

"I said don't let me down on this one."

"Right." He shook his head to clear it. "I'm on my way."

Signing off, he made short work of showering and shaving, then pulled on a pair of khaki slacks and a brown polo shirt. He slung his leather jacket over his shoulder with one hand and used the other to scoop up his keys, making a fist that pressed the sharp metal edges into his palm.

He and the doc needed to get a few things straight.

Molly shifted from foot to foot, the thin stream of heat drifting from the overhead vents in the hangar doing little to warm the icy apprehension in her chest. She'd heard about the uproar she'd caused. But she'd had no idea a few stray words to Doug would come back to bite her.

She wouldn't have said anything if she hadn't been so hurt that Blake didn't want her back on his plane. He'd actually *asked* to be replaced. Had she been *that* terrible during the flight?

Yes.

She'd been nursing her bruised ego when Doug had come up behind her at the hospital and asked if she was looking forward to the flight. The hurt and anger had somehow poured out before she'd had a chance to think about what she was saying. Her friend had been furious on her behalf. But she'd had no idea he'd done anything crazy.

Then again, this was Doug Porter. Crazy was his middle name.

Oh, no, Blake had to be furious.

He had every right to be. Despite the chill lingering deep in her bones, her back-and-forth pacing—along with a bad case of the jitters—had caused a fine sheen of sweat to break out over her body. Shrugging out of her down jacket but leaving on the sweater beneath it, she reached down to unzip her overnight bag, stuffing the garment inside.

Blake had offered to set her up with someone else, but the thought of yet another pilot watching her go into a panic as they took off made her cringe. And what if they ran into another storm? She distinctly remembered a high-pitched keening noise ricocheting around the interior of the cabin.

Yes. Hadn't *that* been lovely?

No wonder he wanted to be rid of her. But it still hurt. And he probably hated her even more now that he was once again stuck with babysitter duty. Why, oh, why hadn't Doug kept his big mouth shut?

Except, deep inside, she had to admit she was glad Blake was taking her and not another pilot. She trusted him. He might have daredevil blood flowing through his veins, but he'd proved there was a limit to the number of risks he was willing to take. He'd refused to take off during the storm that had caused Jed's injury, despite her urging to the contrary—*what had she been thinking?*—which meant he didn't take his job lightly. He wasn't just in it for the thrills, despite his cocky words to the contrary. He wanted to come back from each flight alive.

That made him very attractive in her eyes.

Anyone else was just a big question mark. She knew herself well enough to realize the less she left to chance, the better equipped she'd be to handle future flights and to kick her fear in the teeth and send it skidding down the road.

The door across the room opened and Blake strode in. Without a hint of hesitation he headed straight for her. The only thing in his hand was a jacket, which was slung over his shoulder. And a big frown between his brows.

Uh-oh.

Her elbows pressed close to her body—hands clasped in front—as she tried to prepare herself for the inevitable explosion.

He stopped in front of her. Every inch of his six-foot-three frame vibrated with anger. "Why?"

The word was deadly soft.

His dark shirt hugged his muscular frame, the color bringing out chocolate highlights in his hair. It might have been a warm and comforting combination—if not for his eyes. They held a chill that made her want to take a step backward. She resisted the temptation.

"I know you're upset, but believe me—"

"Why me?" he repeated.

"It was a misunderstanding."

"Oh, I think I understood everything quite well. I was told to get my ass back to Anchorage, and here I am."

"I swear it wasn't me who made that call. It was a friend of mine. But…" How could she explain this without sounding like some kind of loon? "I was hoping you'd reconsider and agree to fly me."

"Why?"

They were back to his initial question. One she wasn't sure she had the answer to. "Because I know you, maybe?"

His brows went up.

"Okay, so I don't *know* you, know you. But I've been on your plane. I've seen you in action. The thought of having a different pilot so soon in the game…" She paused. "I need time to adjust to being in the air before tossing another variable into the mix."

"Another variable?"

"Like a new pilot." She took a deep breath of courage and forced herself to continue. "Someone who might spread stuff around the clinic. I have to be able to get on that plane every time we medevac someone off the island. I need patients to trust that I'll do my very best to care for them while we're in the air. And I will. I *can* set my fear aside, I know I can. Please. Just give my nerves a chance to settle down."

His eyes softened a fraction. "How do you know I won't say anything to anyone?"

"You were at the hospital for several hours the other night when we brought Jed in. After you left, I waited for the whispering or wisecracks to start up. They never did. Even your friend Mark didn't seem to know what happened during that storm. And if you didn't tell him…"

He stiffened. "I didn't talk about the flight, if that's what you mean. I figure it's your business, unless you put someone at risk." He paused. "If that happens, I won't hesitate."

"I wouldn't expect anything less." She unclasped her hands and touched his arm for a second, hoping against hope he'd agree to be her pilot. "So what do you say? Will you take me to Dutch Harbor? Maybe I can earn my first set of wings this time."

She shivered, the chill in the hangar hitting her all at once. Blake's leather jacket somehow wound up draped over her shoulders. The warmth and scent of his body embraced her in a rush. She swallowed, glancing up at him in question.

"You looked cold." A few more slivers of ice melted from his eyes. "And I've got to get my bag out of the car and turn in a flight plan."

She grabbed the edges of his jacket and burrowed deeper into it, trying to make it appear nonchalant.

He had his bag in the car. Which meant he was going to take her!

Doing a happy dance right in front of him would probably not endear her to him. Instead she stood very still. "Thank you."

"You might want to wait until we get there to say that." He stared at the far side of the hangar before glancing back at her. "And in case you're worried about someone at the clinic finding out, don't be. You'll find I'm good at keeping secrets."

Molly breathed a sigh of relief once her feet were back on solid ground. The flight to the Aleutians had been less traumatic this time. At least she hadn't cried or screamed. That had to count for something. She'd still gripped her seat and closed her eyes during takeoff, and her heart had threatened to claw its way out of her chest during landing, but there'd been no storms. No wind. No big "construction zones." Just clear skies.

And Blake.

Two weeks without seeing him should have dampened the attraction. And if that hadn't worked, the reality of passing Gary in the hospital parking lot two days before she was supposed to leave should have snapped her back to her senses. His glower had told her in no uncertain terms that going back to a professional relationship—ever—would be impossible. Getting involved with a medevac pilot would be a very, very bad move on her part. Gary's I'll-get-even attitude had played a big part in her decision to move to the Aleutians. How much worse would it have been if he'd been a pilot—one she had to work with on a regular basis?

Molly shuddered. She really didn't want to go through that again.

Standing on the tarmac beside Blake, she looked out over the water in the distance, trying to compose herself. "Sammi got a line on a rental place for me. She said the outside could use a little work—it doubled as a private business, evidently— but it's nice enough inside and the landlord has promised to paint over the sign out front."

He put his arms behind his head and stretched. A couple of ligaments popped along his back in the process, bringing a smile to her face despite her best efforts. "A sign? Did she tell you where the place is?"

"Nope, she's supposed to go over with me at lunchtime." She took a deep breath. The mixture of chilly air and briny tang burned along her sinuses, but it wasn't unpleasant. Far from it. She wrapped her arms around her waist, as a sense of freedom swept over her.

"Did you bring a coat?"

"I stuffed it in my overnight case while I was waiting at the airport. I didn't have a chance to pull it out before you gave me yours."

"You might need it later. It's pretty mild for Dutch Harbor this time of year. Autumn can be brutal, as you saw on our last trip."

"I remember." His remark brought Mark and the accident at the dockyard to mind. "Did Jed and the girls make it home?"

"I flew them back last week."

"Is he doing okay?"

"I went by on Friday, he seems to be hanging in there. I was planning to check on him again today."

"Do you mind if I go with you? It'll give me a chance to see how his leg is doing. I'm not due to start at the clinic until tomorrow."

"Not a problem."

There'd been a quick hesitation before he'd answered that made her blink. "Are you sure?"

"Absolutely." No pause this time.

"Thanks. How about Mark? Did he get back as well?"

Blake's eyes shifted to her face. "He did."

His voice held some kind of weird tension, but she forced herself to ignore it. Instead, she let the calmness of the ocean act as a soothing balm. After the frenetic couple of weeks she'd spent tying up loose ends in her personal life and at the hospital, she needed some peace and quiet. Scratch that. She'd gotten plenty of quiet at her mother's house as she'd packed her things and got them ready for the movers, but it had been the kind of silence you dreaded.

She didn't have to worry about that any more. "It'll feel good to get settled in. Hopefully we won't have any medevacs for the next couple of days." A sudden thought hit her when she remembered his irritation at the airport this morning and the strange way he was acting now. "Did I pull you away from something? From someone? I never thought to ask."

Her stomach squirmed. She knew from the grapevine he wasn't dating anyone at the hospital, but Anchorage was a big city. And there was always Unalaska. The thought of him kissing someone goodbye cast a pall over her day.

"Nope. Just my bed."

Her heart took a little swan dive, giving her a happy wave as it did.

Get a hold of yourself, Molly. That doesn't mean he's un-attached. For all you know, there might have been someone lying in that bed.

"Sorry about that," she said.

Of course, maybe he really was single.

Forget it. Hadn't she just finished ticking off all the reasons why dating a coworker would not be a smart idea?

Besides, her mother would have a stroke if she got involved with a pilot. She was already upset that Molly's job involved flying of any sort. *Isn't it enough that I've already lost one person to that profession?*

Although if her mother could see the way Blake's tight hindquarters filled out those khakis...

Ack! Steam filtered into her face. She had *not* just noticed his butt.

Her eyes snuck another quick peek. Okay, so maybe she'd glanced a time or two. But that was what girls did. They looked at men's behinds.

Enough was enough. Clearing her throat, she said, "Mind if we swing by the clinic on the way to Jed's? I want to let Sammi know we made it and double-check with her about the rental place. I'm hoping the landlord is willing to do a twelve-month lease with an option to increase it, if I stay."

Blake shoved his hands into his pockets. "If you stay. When will you know?"

"I signed a one-year contract with the clinic, so I need to honor that. If I decide it's not for me, I'm hoping Alaska Regional will send another doctor in my place."

Yeah. She could always dream. What doctor would want to come to a public clinic for what the government wanted to pay? Her advantage was she didn't have a family to support. Just herself.

"Right." He turned away from the water. "You ready to head out?"

"Whenever you are."

The trip to the clinic took just a minute or two, which was a good thing because Blake didn't seem all that inclined to talk. Maybe he was tired after his flight.

Or maybe he was thinking about how long a year would be if she continued to be chicken about flying.

Going through the doors, she caught Sammi just as she was picking up a chart from the receptionist.

The other woman smiled. "Good, you made it." She glanced at the folder in her hand. "Listen, I know I said I'd run you over to the property today, but I have a lunch appointment. One of my prenatal patients, Mindy Starling, is experiencing some Braxton-Hicks contractions, and I want to run over to make sure nothing else is going on."

"Don't worry about—"

Sammi interrupted her with a wave of her hand, glancing at Blake. "Do you mind showing her where it is? I have the keys and the address. The landlord needs a decision by tomorrow morning. He evidently has someone else who's interested if Molly doesn't want it. But don't worry—he's been threatened with bodily harm if he lets the place go before she sees it."

"I need to see what's on the schedule for today."

Sammi grinned. "I already called the station. They can do without you for the rest of the day."

"Thanks. I appreciate that." Blake's tone was even, but he sounded anything but appreciative.

"If you give me the address, maybe I can find it on my own." There was no way she was going to drag him over there against his will.

"Blake doesn't mind. Do you, Blake?"

He gave her a tight smile. "Not at all. We can check on Jed on the way over."

"Great!" Sammi passed an envelope across the countertop. "Call me and let me know what you think."

Well, wasn't this great? Not only had Blake been forced to fly her to Dutch Harbor today, he'd just been volunteered to drag her around half the island. The man had to be thrilled with his lot in life. She was.

Actually, she was. This was her chance to strike out on her own and make her own decisions.

Now, if she could just convince everyone around her to get with the program, she'd be in business.

Jed's place was a wreck.

And from Molly's quick intake of breath, he wasn't the only one who thought so.

Jed, propped on a sofa, his entire leg encased in a cast—no walking boot for a while, according to the orthopedic surgeon—waved them in. "The girls will be sorry they missed you. They only have half a day of school today, so they get out at one. Mark's bringing them home."

Blake glanced at his watch, his muscles relaxing when he noted the time. Eleven-thirty. They'd be gone well before one o'clock.

Molly used her toe to nudge aside a stack of newspapers that had burrowed into the ratty shag carpeting beside the couch before she reached for Jed's wrist and checked her watch. "Do you have someone helping out around here?"

"My sister's bringing in meals, but she's got her own place to take care of." He glanced around, a frown settling between his brows. "And my brother's having to take on extra work over at the dockyard, since I'm out of commission for a while."

Blake could see the wheels spinning in Molly's head as she measured the man's pulse. She was going to spruce up the house. And since he was slated to take her over to the rental property after they left here, he was stuck.

Ah, hell. The last thing Blake wanted to do was stick around and watch his buddy put the moves on Molly. Mark had already mentioned asking her out on more than one occasion, giving Blake a good-natured poke in the ribs as he'd said it. The light-hearted rivalry they'd engaged in as young bachelors no longer seemed all that funny. "Didn't Sammi say someone else was interested in that rental?"

She made a little sound that could be taken as either a yes or a no—depending on one's anxiety level—and began straightening up the end table. He evidently hadn't succeeded in turning this particular plane around.

"I don't have to give them an answer until tomorrow. We have plenty of time," she said.

Plenty of time.

That was exactly what he was afraid of.

CHAPTER SEVEN

SHE'D never seen a man move so fast. Ever.

Even the vacuum cleaner seemed to be huffing and puffing by the time Blake stopped his jerky movements. In less than an hour he'd swept the floors, dusted, straightened the living room and bedroom, and washed a tower of dirty dishes.

Molly looked at what she'd accomplished: making two twin beds and cleaning two bathrooms. She felt like a slug.

He peered around the corner, catching her emptying the trashcan. "Ready?"

That was the third time he'd asked the same question. "What's the big hurry?"

"Just thought you were anxious to see the rental house. At this rate we won't make it before dark."

Her brows went up. "It's not even one yet. Do you have somewhere you need to be?"

He froze, then said, "No. But you can never tell what the weather here is going to do."

"True." She had experienced that firsthand.

Going back into the living room, she checked on Jed. His eyes opened when she touched his forehead, although it was hard to believe he'd been able to sleep with the way Blake had been slinging things around. "Can I fix you a sandwich? I noticed there's some lunchmeat in the fridge."

Blake, who'd followed her into the room, groaned. *Out*

loud! She sent him a quick glare. What was wrong with the man?

Her patient shrugged. "My sister should be around pretty soon. She'll slap something together for me."

"Why don't you call and let her know you've already eaten? She could probably use a little down time. I'll leave something in the fridge for the girls as well."

Jed shifted on the couch. "I don't want to put you out, Doc. Blake's right. You've got other things to do."

"That's all right. Blake's going to help me get those sandwiches ready. In the kitchen." She sent him a pointed glance. "We'll be right back."

When it didn't look like he was going to follow her, she grabbed the hem of his shirt and dragged him with her. Once they turned the corner she released her hold and whipped around to face him. "Like I said, if you have somewhere else you need to be, don't let me stop you. I can call a cab and make it to the house on my own."

"I don't have anywhere to be. You heard Sammi. I have the whole day off." He crossed his arms over his chest.

"Then what's with all the little impatient sounds?"

"I haven't been making…"

Her hands went to her hips, cutting off his denial. Dull color crept up his neck.

Molly opened the fridge and pulled out a pack of lunchmeat and cheese. "You want to make some coffee while I do this?"

He paused, then took a step closer, taking the packages out of her hand and placing them on the counter. "I always seem to make a fool of myself when you're around, don't I?"

"Not *always*." She softened the words with a smile. "My dad said you have to be careful about using absolutes."

And although she held onto the smile, it faded away inside.

Her mother had often used those exact things when throwing accusations at him.

You always... You never... Why don't you ever...?

Her father had often caught her mother by the shoulders when she'd been in one of her moods and looked into her face. *Be careful with those absolutes, Hannah.* More often than not, his words had stopped her mother in her tracks. At least until the year before he'd died. Then he'd grown more distant and his absences longer, according to her mother.

"Come again?" Blake's question brought her back.

"Nothing." A warning tingle hovered behind her eyes. *Tears.*

She missed her father terribly all of a sudden. Turning quickly, she made her way over to the breadbox and peered inside, using those precious seconds to will away the moisture.

A hand covered hers, closing the box before tugging her around to face him. His eyes roamed her face, a frown settling between his brows.

"Hey. I didn't mean to upset you."

She shook her head, unable to answer.

Still wrapped around her wrist, his fingers tightened a fraction. He pulled her against his chest just as the first hot tear overflowed her eyelids before being absorbed into his shirt.

"Shh." His hand slid over her back. "I'm sorry, Molly."

She tried to shake her head and let him know this wasn't about him, but he just pressed her closer. Taking a deep shuddering breath, she tilted her head back and glanced up at him. "It's not you. I—I just…" The words wouldn't come. She swallowed and tried again. "I wish he hadn't…"

Comprehension dawned in his eyes. "Your dad?"

She nodded, grateful she didn't need to say anything more.

His index finger teased a strand of hair off her temple before trailing down her cheek. "I know. I miss him too."

Something welled in her chest. The need for the comfort of a fellow human being, surely. Yes, there was that, but something else hummed along beside it as his warm touch moved to her jaw and stroked gently, leaving prickles of sensation in its wake.

"I'm sorry for blubbering all over you."

"It's okay." His fingers slowed as something in his gaze changed, heated. Her breath caught.

The hand at her jaw moved back, curving around her nape, his thumb settling against the underside of her chin. He used it to apply gentle pressure to tilt her head farther back.

His gaze settled on her mouth. Oh, man, was he going to kiss her?

Unable to stop herself, she licked her suddenly parched lips.

"Molly." The word was whispered. A statement, not a question, but she heard the request nonetheless.

She opened her mouth to answer when a voice came from the other room. "You two okay out there?"

Blake stepped back as if shot in the chest, his hand falling away from her face. He looked toward the doorway, clearing his voice. "We're fine. Just getting things together."

It was going to take a few seconds to do just that: get herself together.

What was she thinking? This was crazy. She needed to stop this before it was too late.

Rather than attempt to speak, she gathered the rest of the sandwich makings in silence, not daring to look at him.

He must have been doing the same thing because she heard the sound of water hitting the bottom of some kind of receptacle. A minute or two later the scent of fresh coffee drifted by her nose as she sliced the roast-beef sandwiches she'd made into diagonal halves.

Rummaging through the refrigerator, she was glad to find

a supply of fresh-looking apples in the fruit bin. His sister's work, probably. She took a couple out and cut them into slices, putting some of them on the plate with Jed's sandwich. She tossed the rest of the slices with a bit of lemon water to keep them from turning brown and put the bowl in the refrigerator for the girls. "How do you like your coffee, Jed?" she called.

"Black and strong."

She glanced in Blake's direction and found him looking back at her. He held up a mug, indicating it was ready.

"Let me see if I can find a tray," she said.

Behind the cabinet doors she found nothing but a motley array of dishes, as well as pots and pans.

"I saw a set of TV trays in the front room. If you'll carry his plate and a napkin, I'll take in the mug and the coffeepot."

Once they got to the living room, Molly handed Jed the plate and set a metal tray on its feet in front of the couch. "Do you want me to turn on the news?"

"Thanks." He pulled himself a bit more upright, and she bunched the pillow behind him to support his back while Blake set down coffee.

"Why don't you two at least join me for coffee?"

The same impatient look he'd worn earlier slid across Blake's face, but at least there were no accompanying vocalizations to go along with it.

He doesn't want to stay. But why? Does he have something against Jed?

Or was it because of what had just happened between the two of them in the kitchen?

Whatever the reason, she didn't want to push her luck—or her self-control—any further.

"Coffee sounds great, but Sammi found a rental house I need to look at. I did leave some sandwiches and apple slices in the refrigerator for the girls."

The furrows between Blake's eyes disappeared instantly. So it wasn't her imagination.

Jed's glance went from her to Blake. "Thanks for everything you've done."

"You just work on getting better." Molly forced herself to smile at him, trying to forget that Blake would be the one taking her to see that rental house. Soft wings fluttered across her tummy. She and Blake alone? Without Jed or anyone else to interrupt them?

Oh, Lord, why did that prospect excite her?

Get a grip, Molly. Who said Blake was looking for anything? *She* certainly wasn't. She might have even misread his intentions a few minutes ago.

Jed, totally unaware of the thoughts whirling around her head, picked up the sandwich and took a bite. His eyes shut for a second and he gave a low grunt of approval as he savored the bite. "Roast beef with horseradish sauce. How did you know?"

She laughed, glad to be pulled back to the present. "Easy. No one has a half-empty jar of it in their fridge—especially when the expiration date is still ages away—unless they really like it." She gave him a wink. "I should know. I use the very same brand."

When Blake's glance jerked from the sandwich and landed on her, she cocked her head. "What's wrong, flyboy? You prefer something with a little less kick?"

"If by *kick* you mean having my tonsils shoved through the back of my throat, the answer is yes." His eyes narrowed in on her mouth. "Other than that, I like plenty of spice."

His words gave that scene in the kitchen a whole new meaning.

She swallowed, trying to bring some moisture to her suddenly dry throat. "If you've got everything you need, Jed, I'm going to take off. You'll be okay?"

Still chewing, and looking as if he could float away at any minute, he gave an I'll-be-fine wave of his hand.

On the way to the door Molly turned toward him one last time. "Don't forget your meds. And I've left my card on the table. Call my cell if you need me."

At his nod she stepped outside, Blake right on her heels.

He glanced at his watch for the umpteenth time just as a car pulled up in the driveway. Molly thought he swore under his breath when the girls piled out of it, rushing toward her, followed by Mark.

She threw him a funny look before the girls reached her, then she knelt down to embrace each of them. "Hi, you guys! How was school?"

"Great. We got out early because the teachers are making plans."

She laughed. "They are, huh?"

The younger one giggled. "Are you coming to visit Daddy?"

"I already did. I left you some lunch in the refrigerator. Sandwiches and apple slices." She glanced up at Mark. "Would you mind getting the food out for them once you go inside?"

"I'd be happy to." He reached down a hand to help her up. "I'm glad you're back," he murmured.

She smiled, removing her hand from his. "It's definitely good to be back on solid ground."

Mark glanced at Blake, who hadn't said a word. "This guy hasn't been trying any funny stuff, has he?"

"Excuse me?" Shock rolled through her. Had he seen something in her face?

"He likes to pretend he's a stunt pilot from time to time, waving his wings and stuff like that."

"O-oh, no. Nothing like that." Along with a sense of relief came surprise. She couldn't imagine Blake, who'd proved himself to be anything but Evel Knievel-like when in the air, pulling anything crazy. Knowing how her father died, maybe he was being extra-careful when she was on the plane. Although he didn't *always* play it safe, according to Mark.

A shiver went over her.

If anything, that should make her more resolute than ever. Stick to being on a professional footing with Blake, both in the air and on the ground.

As if he'd heard her thoughts, Blake finally spoke up. "Don't you need to get inside? I'm sure Jed's wondering where the girls are."

Mark answered with a lift of his brows before shifting his attention back to Molly. "What are your plans for the next couple of days?"

"I don't know. I'm looking at a house to rent this afternoon, then tomorrow I start at the clinic."

"Sammi doesn't waste any time, does she?" There was a slight edge to Mark's voice that he covered with a smile. "In that case, I need to ask while I have the chance. Are you doing anything for dinner, or has this guy monopolized all your free time?" He hooked a thumb in Blake's direction.

She blinked in surprise. Blake had mentioned he might ask her out.

Opening her mouth to refuse, she stopped short. What better way to get it through her own thick skull that she wasn't interested in a serious relationship?

Mark is kind of a ladies' man. Blake's words came back to her. If that was true, she didn't have to worry about him taking things too seriously. They could go out and have a good time. No strings attached. And Blake would know she wasn't looking to him to entertain her…in any way. "I don't have plans."

Blake shifted beside her, but she didn't look his way. The girls were starting to get impatient as well, grabbing at Mark's hand and trying to pull him toward the front door of the house.

"Great. How about a quick dinner then I can show you what Unalaska has to offer?"

"Sounds good."

"I'll pick you up, say, at seven?" He allowed himself to be dragged away, calling over his shoulder, "Where are you staying?"

"At the UniSea."

"See you there."

With that, the trio disappeared through the door of the house, leaving her alone with Blake. When she finally dared to look his way, his face was blank, not a hint of emotion crossing it. Disappointment filtered through her.

Guess you didn't need to get your point across after all, Molly. The man isn't interested.

"Do you have the address?"

"Somewhere." Molly fished around in her purse, until she found the envelope with the key. The address was typed across the top. "118 North Wharf Drive."

"I know where the street is. It's not too far from here."

Neither one of them mentioned what had happened at Jed's house or Mark's dinner invitation. Maybe it was better this way.

Heat crawled over her face. And yet if Blake had kissed her back at Jed's she wouldn't have turned away. How could she have faced him after that?

Thank God none of it had happened. And by accepting Mark's invitation, she'd made sure it never would.

"The street should be right around…"

Molly spotted the sign. "There. Off to your right."

"I see it." He made the turn into a modest residential area, the clapboard houses adorned in a wide array of pastel colors. "What was the number again?"

"One-eighteen." Her eyes scoured the buildings. "The even numbers are on the right."

"Three hundred block, so we're close."

"There. The light blue house."

Pulling into the gravel driveway, she noted the "For Rent" sign pushed into grass that was just starting to turn brown. Blake made a strangled sound.

"What's wrong?" Her voice drifted away as she stared at the front of the house. Sammi had said the outside needed a little work, but she didn't notice any of that. She couldn't. Her eyes refused to budge from the words stenciled in bold black letters across the left portion of the building.

SCENTS OF PLEASURE: AROMATHERAPY AND MASSAGE OILS.

CHAPTER EIGHT

"I BET that was really popular with the neighbors."

Molly pulled herself together. "Very funny. Sammi did mention something about a sign needing to be painted over."

"Are you sure you want to do that? You could start a little side business of your own."

She leveled a glare at him. "Did you know this was here?" If so, he could have at least warned her. Maybe that was why he'd acted so funny at Jed's house.

"No, I've never had the pleasu—" He stopped when he saw the look on her face. "No. I had no idea."

He must have realized she wasn't finding any of this amusing, because he squeezed the hand that lay between them on the seat. "I'm sure it's fine. Sammi said the inside was nice, right?"

"I hope so." She pulled the key out of the envelope. "Do you want to stay here while I take a look?" Part of her hoped he would, afraid she might find something other than essential oils and innocent massage items inside.

"This is a nice neighborhood, but I'll go with you, just in case."

They made their way to the door and Molly unlocked it. She then moved aside to let Blake go first, praying he was right and there was nothing kinky inside. A painfully normal foyer met her eyes.

Thank you.

No oils with suggestive names. No "personal" massagers standing at attention.

In fact, the place was nice. Really nice. The living room had creamy white paneling and soft taupe carpet that looked and smelled freshly cleaned. White roman shades were all at half-mast, allowing her to see how bright and airy the place would be during the day.

"This is wonderful. Far better than I imagined."

"Looks like you're hitting a home run at every turn today." The wry tone made her glance up quickly, wondering if he was making a crack about her date with Mark. Nothing in his face seemed to indicate he was making fun of her, though. "It's not always easy to find a decent place to rent. Housing is tight on the islands."

"Oh." She started to move to the next room when a slapping sound came from somewhere in the back of the house. She sucked in a breath, gooseflesh prickling along her arms. "Did you hear that?"

"Stay here." The low words slid past her ear, sending another shiver over her.

Before he could move, a white furry head peered around the corner. Her brain didn't have a chance to process what it was. She automatically cringed sideways, knocking into Blake, who grabbed her to keep her from dragging both of them to the floor.

"Easy, it's just a cat."

A cat. Not a mouse or other creepy-crawly.

She shuddered. "Thank God." Her breath rattled in her chest as she tried to find her composure. Problem was, it was nowhere in sight. Something touched the top of her head, and she realized her side was still pressed tight against Blake's front, his arms wrapped around her, warm breath ruffling her hair—breath that sounded almost as unsteady as her own. The world tilted slightly as he murmured, "You okay?"

She opened her mouth to answer, but nothing came out, her mind zeroing in on each contact point between their bodies and trying to decipher body parts. Chin against top of head. *Check.* Hard chest wall touching right shoulder blade. *Check.* Her right hip against his… *Yikes.*

Clearing her throat and using it as an excuse to pull away, she stuffed her hands in the pockets of her jacket, looking anywhere but at him. "I'm fine. It just startled me."

Blake was right. A cat with dusty white fur and a blue collar inched farther into the room, staring at them with wary eyes. She was surprised the animal hadn't turned around and run away

"Poor thing. I wonder how it got in?" She knelt and called to it softly, holding out her hand.

"I don't know." Blake moved through to the area they'd heard the sound. "There's a pet door back here," he called. He reappeared a minute later.

"Do you think the previous tenant left her behind?" The cat rubbed against her hand, purring softly. "Surely not."

"She knows how to get in." The cat gave a little meow. "She looks well fed, too. Maybe the landlord knows how to contact the people who used to live here."

"I'm supposed to give him an answer tomorrow, but I'm not sure what to do with her until then. I suppose I could keep her as long as the landlord is okay with it. The house doesn't smell bad, so hopefully she's litter trained." She scrubbed under the cat's chin and laughed when the animal tilted its head back a little farther.

The softness of Molly's face as she stroked the cat caused his heart to give a couple of hard thumps in his chest. He stiffened, remembering his lapse a few minutes earlier. When she'd stumbled against him, his instinctual reaction had been to keep her from falling. That primal urge to protect had been short-lived and followed by something else entirely. The scent of her hair had intoxicated him and he hadn't been able to resist leaning closer, his chin coming in for a landing on the top of her head. And those soft curves.

He tried to throw off the sensations, but they hung around the periphery, waiting to pounce on him when he least expected it.

She's going out with Mark. She's made her choice.

As if he were even in the running. No way. He'd taken himself out of that particular race long ago. So why had he allowed himself to get close enough to settle his head against hers? Because it was what he used to do with Sharon? An instinctive reaction?

Maybe, except Molly was a brunette, not a blonde. And her warm scent didn't fill him with memories of shouting matches followed by bitter periods of silence.

Her voice was nothing like Sharon's either. Molly's low, breathy tones turned his gut completely inside out and wiped out any higher cortical activity. Right now, it was brainstem all the way. That made her dangerous. And, oh, so tempting all at the same time.

"She's so sweet." Molly had picked the cat up by this time, holding her in her arms. The cat rubbed the top of her head against Molly's chin. "She's definitely not afraid of me."

Blake, on the other hand, was shaking in his boots. "Maybe we should finish looking at the house." He needed a good reason to get out of this building before he did anything stupid. Like he'd almost done at Jed's. He was a thread away from repeating that mistake, Mark or no Mark.

"Okay." Setting the cat on the floor, they waited to see what she would do. She just stood there twisting her head from side to side as she looked from one to the other. "I guess she's not going anywhere for the moment."

They quickly toured the rest of the house, which Molly liked as much as the living room. "I think I'm going to take it."

"Cat and all?"

"I can't very well kick her out, if she's used to being here. Maybe I can find her owner." She put her hands on her hips. "Or at least a litter box."

She wanted the cat to stay. He could hear it in her voice. Something inside him melted. He clenched his teeth, willing himself not to say the words, but they came out anyway. "I could always put her up at my place until you get your furniture and things settled. At least you'd know she was fed and safe."

"Are you serious?"

What the hell was wrong with him? He should have let Mark offer to take the thing in. He was the one interested in Molly, not him.

Except his friend was allergic to cats…had sneezed every time he'd come face-to-face with his mom's cat when he'd come over to the house. A slow smile came over his face.

"Definitely."

Her hand touched his. "Thank you. Maybe we'll find her owner."

"Maybe. I'll bring a crate over later and take her home and feed her. Once you get settled, you can come by and get her."

Her fingers curled around his. "You won't regret this."

He should regret it. He should make an effort to dredge up some semblance of that elusive emotion. Instead, all he wanted to do was kiss Molly until she couldn't breathe. And that was impossible. Not only because it wasn't a smart thing to do.

But because Mark had already made his move and had, in effect, snatched Molly right out of his hands.

CHAPTER NINE

INSTEAD of heading to the hotel, Molly decided to go back to the clinic to give Sammi the news about the house and see how things had gone with her pregnant patient.

She was also anxious to get to work. While she could make good money in private practice, that wasn't why she'd gone into medicine.

So here were her current challenges: surviving the flights to and from the islands and working hard to prove the government dollars were well spent. If she could do those two things, hopefully the work would continue, even if she couldn't.

"Did you like it?" Sammi tossed her long braid over her shoulder.

"It was beautiful! I'm going to take it."

"What about that sign? Wasn't it a hoot?"

Molly grimaced. "Yeah, especially having a man in the car with me when I got there."

"Hey, you never know. Blake's quite a catch, if you haven't noticed."

She glanced away. "Really? He seems kind of standoffish to me." Picking a chart up from the counter, she flipped it open as if reading it. "Besides, Mark asked me out, and *he* is rather yummy, don't you think?"

A second or two of silence went by and Molly looked up

to find Sammi on the other side of the room, staring out the window. She frowned. "Is everything okay?"

"Yep." The other woman turned around with a smile. "Tell Mark I said hi when you see him. In the meantime, could you give me a hand? I have two patients waiting and the PA is off for the rest of the day."

"Sure." Something about Sammi seemed artificially bright all of a sudden, but she couldn't place exactly what it was that made her think so. So she accepted the file handed to her and went to the exam room the CHA indicated.

A half hour later she swiveled on the stool to face Sarah, her five-year-old patient, gently wrapping an ace bandage around the child's wrist. "It's not broken according to the X-ray, but it still must hurt, huh?"

The little girl's breath hitched as it had several times during the exam, and she clutched her mother's hand. "Uh-huh."

"No more bike riding for the next week or so, okay?"

Sniffling, Sarah leaned against her mother, who stroked her hair and said, "Your arm will be as good as new in no time. You'll see."

Molly nodded. "That's right." She rummaged through a couple of drawers until she found a stash of slings with the clinic's initials inscribed on the outside. Sorting through them, she found one she hoped would fit Sarah's small arm. Maybe the device would also remind the girl why she couldn't ride her bike. She went over to the table and positioned Sarah's limb. "Can you hold your arm here while I put this on?"

The sling went on easily, with no fuss. Afterward, Sarah touched it with her other hand. "It's pink, just like my bike."

"See, isn't that better? You need to wear it until your next appointment." She gave the child's mother a wink and held up crossed fingers, hoping she'd realize the sling was just a prop. Then she helped the child climb off the table.

Sarah's mom mouthed, "Thank you."

"Can I have a lollipop? Sammi always gives me one, 'cause I'm a good girl."

And cheeky, too.

She glanced around the room. "Do you know where she keeps them?"

"She hides them inside there, behind a bunch of junk..." Sarah pointed at one of the upper cabinets "...but all the kids know where they are."

The haughty tilt of her nose said the adults around this place had gravely underestimated their young patients.

The child's mom gave her daughter a warning frown. "Sarah..."

Laughing, Molly went to the cabinet and slid her hand deep into its recesses. Sure enough, toward the back was a large round-bellied Mason jar. When she pulled it forward, a colorful array of treats met her eyes. A big label on the side divided the sweets according to color and what they were intended to reward. Nifty idea.

Red: Valor.

Green: Broken bones.

Yellow: Sunny disposition.

Purple: Vaccinations.

Orange: Courage.

Blue: Stitches.

She pulled it off the shelf and set it on the counter. "Now let's see which one you've earned."

"The blue one stains your tongue."

Molly's brows went up. "It does?" She glanced at the label. "You've had stitches before?"

"No, but sometimes Sammi lets kids choose the color." The little girl leaned closer, her eyes round. "Even if they cry."

"Does she? Sammi's a very nice lady, to let you do that."

An energetic nod followed.

They'd evidently made their fair share of trips to the clinic.

Molly was glad she'd come. Maybe Sammi wouldn't be run as ragged as she'd evidently been the past couple of months.

"So which color do you think you've earned?" She popped open the latch that held the glass lid in place. The scent of sugar wafted up, despite the plastic wrapping around each individual pop.

Sarah studied the label, her lips pursed. "My bone's not broken, right?"

"Right." Molly gave her mother a quick smile. Choosing a sucker was serious business around these parts.

"I was brave, though, wasn't I?"

"Very."

"But the blue…" The child's wistful eyes searched the jar, obviously looking for something.

Molly spun the glass container around. There was only one blue left. That staining feature Sarah had mentioned hadn't made it any less popular. In fact, it appeared to be the most desirable lollipop on the block.

"I think we can make an exception in this case, since you were so brave about letting me X-ray that arm."

"Really?"

"Absolutely." She crooked an arm around the jar and tilted the mouth of it toward the child. "I'll even let you reach in and get it, if you want. It's on the very bottom, though, do you think you can manage it with your left hand?"

"I'm left-handed." The pride in her voice was obvious, bringing another smile to Molly's face.

"Well, there you go."

Tiny fingers wiggled their way through the sea of lollipops until her whole arm was swallowed by the jar's neck. Once she reached the sweet and pulled it out, her mother draped a hand over Sarah's shoulder. "What do you say?"

"Thank you," she said in that cute sing-songy tone children used when responding to a prompt.

"You're very welcome." Molly glanced at her watch. She should probably head back to the hotel. Hopefully Blake had been able to catch the cat. The thought of seeing him again brought a strange little rush of pleasure to her tummy.

Not good.

You've only known the man a little while.

But the fizzy sensation remained, undaunted by the internal reprimand.

Sarah's voice came back through. "Can I eat it now, Mommy?"

"After lunch."

"Can't it be an appet…an apperti…" She searched for the word. "Apperitizer?"

"Appetizer. And, no, it can't. It'll be dessert, which comes *after* we eat."

The girl's lower lip moved back into a threatening position, and her mom gave a little laugh. "Come on, time to go."

Waving as the pair headed out the door, Molly turned back to the room so she could tidy up. She pulled the paper covering the exam table through the feed at the bottom until the surface was covered with a fresh, clean layer, ripping off the used portion and wadding it in a ball. As she turned to toss it into a nearby trashcan, she almost jumped out of her skin when she found Blake standing in the doorway.

"What are you doing here?"

"I wanted to let you know that the cat walked right into the crate as if she'd been in one before. She's already at my house, chowing down on some food. Anyway, Sammi said you had a patient. I didn't want to interrupt you, so I waited." He helped himself to a piece of candy from the jar.

A giddy little laugh came out, and she cleared her throat, trying for a frown instead. She glanced at his hand. "Yellow. Really?"

"Huh?"

She tapped a finger to Sammi's labeling system, hoping to ward off the crazy sensations that were rising in her chest. "Things like that have to be earned."

He squinted at the notations. "Sunny disposition. That describes me to a T."

"Right."

"Besides," he said, "the blue ones appear to be all gone."

She rolled her eyes. "Not you, too."

"Hey, if you can't beat 'em…"

He actually was in kind of a sunny mood. Surprising. What had cheered him up? "So the cat seems to be okay?"

"She's fine. I went ahead and checked with the vet in town. No one seems to be missing her."

He propped a hip against the counter, evidently in no hurry to leave.

As for her, she needed to get back to the hotel and get ready for her date. Anything to avoid standing here staring at Blake.

She opened the chart and began writing up her notes. "I got the rental by the way. I sign the contract in the morning."

"Good to hear. When are you moving in?"

"I'll be at the hotel another couple of days until my things arrive. Probably on Thursday or Friday."

"Hmm."

She snuck a glance at where he was methodically flipping the sucker, catching it by the stick on every second twirl. His biceps—seemingly oblivious to the actual weight of the candy—responded as if it were dealing with a two-ton barbell, tightening into a solid mass of muscle with every toss. Tearing her eyes away took discipline and courage. Two things she lacked right now.

Yeah, she was a professional all right.

"I've still got your things in the back of my car. How do you want to work this?"

Ah, so that's why he was still here. Man, she was dense sometimes.

"I'd totally forgotten about the suitcases. Sorry."

So how *did* she want to handle this? She didn't have a vehicle yet. Maybe Sammi could—

"I could give you a lift to the hotel and drop the stuff off."

Relief swept over her. "That would be great, thanks. I'll see about getting a rental car tomorrow."

She finished jotting her notes, and glanced at the previous ones to see if Sammi had a specific format she wanted followed.

Yep. She'd recorded the color of each sucker for each visit. Curious, she thumbed through the entries. Red. Red. Blue. Yellow. Blue. Blue. Blue.

Molly laughed as she penned blue at the end of her own notes. That made four blues in a row.

"What?"

"Just thinking about how people—even kids—get on a kick and don't want to move away from it."

"Not sure I follow you."

"My patient's favorite lollipop was blue."

"Which means?"

She shrugged. "Even at a young age, we as humans start digging a rut for ourselves and then settling into it. The deeper we dig, the harder it is to climb back out." She reached in the jar and pulled out a lollipop, staring at it for a moment. Holding it upside down, she made a couple of scooping motions. "You can make a shovel out of almost anything if you try hard enough. Even a simple piece of candy."

"I still don't follow."

Maybe that had been part of the reason her parents' marriage had floundered. They'd allowed themselves to settle into an unhealthy routine that had gotten deeper and deeper until they'd been trapped. And her own relationships had followed a similar course. She'd worked harder and harder to please Gary—and her mother—but it had never been enough. She'd just kept digging. Until she'd finally thrown down her shovel and scrambled up out of that hole.

"I was just thinking about my mom and dad, and how they argued about his job. How my mom always tore my dad down. It's hard for people to change when something's become ingrained."

She closed the chart, noting Blake had gone very still. "Something wrong?"

"Just thinking."

She wanted to ask, but it was none of her business, really. To cover up the awkwardness, she worked to put the rest of the room in order. He moved to stand by the wall without needing to be asked when she reached into a cupboard and pulled out a bottle of disinfectant spray. Giving the counter a couple of healthy squirts, she waited a few seconds for the solution to kill any microbes before drying it with a wad of paper towels. Blake remained silent, not even attempting to find a topic of conversation.

Then again, neither did she. She'd evidently said something wrong.

She shut her eyes and realized what it was. He didn't want to hear about her parents' problems. That was something personal, and Molly wasn't even sure why she'd brought the subject up. Blake had worked with her father—had respected him. Why would he want to hear anything that might cast a pall on the man who'd helped train him? Great. Just when she'd thought he was softening, she had to go and mess things up. "I'm almost done."

"No hurry." The words were generous, but the tightness she'd heard at other times was back in his voice. Yep. She'd definitely made some kind of gaffe.

When Sammi poked her head into the room, Molly was

grateful for the interruption. "I just finished with my patient. How'd it go with Sarah?"

"Fine. No breaks. Just a bad sprain. I put her arm in a sling and told her to take it easy for a while."

Sammi's eyes went to the candy jar. "I forgot to tell you about the lollipops."

"Don't worry. Sarah let me know." She refastened the lid. "You're out of blue, by the way."

Sammi laughed. "I should have stuck to the chart. But once I let the kids talk me into breaking tradition, there was no stopping them. Blue is all the rage right now. Kind of like a badge of honor for surviving this place. Maybe I should nix that color."

"I wouldn't do that." To her surprise, Blake spoke up, holding up his sucker. "It's not just the kids who are guilty. I play favorites, too."

"So you're a yellow man."

"It would seem that way." His lips gave a wry twist. "Although, according to Molly, a shovel is a shovel, no matter what the color."

CHAPTER TEN

A RUT is a grave with both ends kicked out.

The quote flashed through Blake's head as he rang Molly's doorbell. Holding the pet crate in one hand, he'd shoved his other one into the pocket of his leather jacket, discovering the still wrapped sucker he'd picked up at the clinic two days ago. He closed his fist around it.

What the hell was he doing here? He'd climbed out of one deep rut, was he really stupid enough to start digging another one? He hadn't seen or heard from Mark since that day at Jed's house—when he'd asked Molly out—so he had no idea how their date had gone.

Neither did he care.

His own failed marriage and Wayne's tale of woe had convinced him it took a man with nerves of steel to be both a bush pilot and a husband. Something he evidently didn't have. Which brought him back to the question of what he was doing here. He could have dropped the cat crate off at the clinic this afternoon and let Molly carry it home herself. But he'd been curious about how things were going with her new place. There'd been no real medical emergencies since he'd been back, nothing to keep his mind off things. So here he was. But as soon as she opened the door, he'd hand her the crate and leave.

And he *would* leave.

He might have to work with Molly on medevacs, but following her around the island hadn't been part of that package.

The door opened, and there she stood in a black stretchy top, a hand towel looped over one shoulder. Music with some kind of thumping beat washed through the opening, making him blink, as did the sight of Molly's teeth coming down on her soft lower lip. She glanced back inside the house, the gap in the doorway narrowing.

Was that guilt?

"Um, hi, I wasn't expecting you."

He frowned. Was Mark here or something?

"Sorry for not calling first. Sammi said you'd already left for the day." Actually, he'd been convinced he could talk himself out of coming over here in person, so he hadn't bothered. But here he was…on her doorstep. "Is this a bad time?"

"No. Come on in. My things arrived from the mainland this morning, but I had to leave for work as soon as they unloaded the truck. The place is a wreck."

"That's okay. I can't stay long." He lifted the crate. "I told you I'd bring her by once you moved in."

As if she'd just noticed what he held, Molly knelt and peered inside the box. "Hey, sweetie. You ready to come home?" She glanced back up. "I asked the landlord about the previous renters, but he said they moved off the island and didn't leave a forwarding address. One of the neighbors felt sorry for her, and had been leaving food out, so I guess she's officially mine." She stood aside to let him come in.

The music grew louder and chaos met him as soon as he reached the living room. Half-opened boxes were scattered around the periphery of the space, with similar items grouped together. A laptop computer, perched on top of one of the boxes belted out a tune from a dance movie, the screen swirling with patterns that kept time with the beat. The center of the room was completely clear, as if a centrifuge had gone on the fritz and blown everything backward.

It was then he noticed Molly's snug, stretchy top was joined by a matching pair of Lycra pants. Exercise gear. And the towel...

She was dancing.

He swallowed. It made sense. The type of music. The light sheen of perspiration dotting her upper lip...the deep scoop of her neckline, which had slid off her left shoulder, revealing a black bra strap.

Realizing he might be staring—*was* staring—and that his lower jaw was probably located somewhere on the carpet beneath his feet, he cleared his throat. Molly hiked the renegade sleeve back over her shoulder and turned the volume down on the music, blushing a deep pink. "I was just..."

"It's okay. No explanation needed." His imagination had filled in every possible blank.

"I—I have coffee made. Do you want some?"

Hell, he wanted something, but it wasn't coffee. "Um, what do you want me to do with...?" He nodded down at the cat crate.

"Oh, right. Poor thing. I'm a little frazzled."

She wasn't the only one. And the more he pictured her writhing in time to that wild rhythm she had going, the warmer he got.

Kneeling in front of him to open the cage, she spoke in soft tones to the cat, coaxing her from the dark recesses of the container. She soon had her in her arms. The feline's head pushed against her chin in greeting. "I've already got some food and litter for her." She laughed at the way the cat snuggled against her, front legs dangling over Molly's forearm as if perched on a familiar ledge.

Blake tried not to picture that cat's white fur sticking to

Molly's black top, or how she might roll a lint brush over those soft curves later. "There are a couple of toys in the crate."

"You bought her toys?"

The throaty whisper transformed the growing heat in his chest into a small blaze. He shrugged, trying to firm his resolve to clear out at the first opportunity. "Just a few. They were on sale."

There, that should sound tough enough.

She smiled. "Blake Taylor, could you have a soft spot for animals?"

Absolutely not.

Even as the protest bounced through his head, he knew it was a lie. The cat had exited the crate at his house, rubbing against his leg and purring up a storm. The animal had looked up at him. And those eyes...

Luminous green. Changing with her moods. Just like Molly's.

"Come and have some coffee while I show her where her litter box is."

The smart thing to do would be to back out of the room and say a quick goodbye. He followed her instead, watching as Molly set the animal next to a litter box she'd stowed in the laundry area. The cat took one look then turned around and stalked off.

"Pets are kind of permanent. Does this mean you're thinking of staying longer than a year?"

"I don't know. Do you think they'll ever build a bridge from the mainland?"

The smile told him it was a joke, but his chest felt tight and strange. "I think you're stuck with flying. You'll get used to it."

Standing, she went to the sink and washed her hands, then took two mugs from a nearby box and rinsed them. "Hmm...

maybe. I don't think I'll ever really *like* flying, but I've proved to myself I can do it. That's all that matters, right?"

The words were like a boot to the chest, knocking the wind from him.

How could something that was so exhilarating to him—something that gave him a huge jolt of satisfaction every time his plane left the ground—produce the exact opposite reaction in someone else?

Oblivious to his thoughts, she said, "Thank you, Blake. It—it means a lot to me that you watched her and that you cared enough to play with her."

Her gaze met his, and he had to force himself not to look away as thoughts of escape crowded in around him. "She wasn't any trouble."

His hand went back to the sucker, gripping tight. Maybe he'd frame the thing as a reminder: the digging stopped right here. Right now.

Regardless of how his gut twisted at having to keep standing there, he stayed put, even when she took a step closer and touched his arm. He swore he could feel the warmth of her palm, even through his thick leather jacket. "You'll stay and have some coffee? As a small token of my thanks?"

"Yes." The word came out as a croak.

He gulped when her fingers tightened slightly. Pinpoints of heat and cold danced across his body, as if some cosmic disco ball was releasing short bursts of energy as it spun round and round. It blinded him to everything but her touch. "You don't need to thank me. You'd do the same for me."

"Maybe. It depends on what I had to do. Fly a plane, for example? Not much chance of that." Her hand slid a little higher, her thumb sweeping a path across his upper arm.

He sucked down a breath, all thoughts of escape evaporating. Was she aware of what her touch was doing to him?

Talk. Don't think.

"Don't sell yourself short. You'd do it, if you had to." His voice came out all scratchy and his throat grew tight, along with other key areas of his body.

"As much as I want to believe that, there's not much chance of me ever attempting it. Not unless you passed out in mid-flight, and even the thought of that happening makes me break out in a cold sweat."

Something niggled at the back of his mind, something other than the wave of lust rushing up his spine demanding to be heard. Even as he fought the urge, he reached toward her, unable to resist touching a lock of that glossy brown hair.

Soft. Silky.

Just as he'd imagined it would be.

When she released a sigh instead of stepping back, he slid his fingers deeper into the shiny strands, letting them sift through his fingertips. No hairspray. Nothing that screamed, *Don't touch.* Just thick, velvety tresses that whispered against his skin.

"I like your hair short like this." Where the words had come from, he had no idea.

"You do?"

His eyes shifted to her lips. Were they as moist and invit-ing as they looked? He could just lean down and…

Almost before he knew what he was doing, his mouth touched hers. Just for a second. He meant to pull away. He was certain of it. Then she tilted her head, her hands going to his shoulders as she pressed closer. She had to be on tip-toe to reach him like that.

She wanted his kiss. Liked it.

Damn. His heart and his mind tussled for a second or two before the primal side kicked the rational to the curb, flip-ping it a bird and sending it scurrying to some dark corner of his mind.

There. That was better.

Molly swayed for a second. To stabilize her—*yeah, that was the reason*—he wrapped one arm around her waist, while the fingers of his other hand remained in her hair, molding themselves to the delicate bones of her skull.

What was he doing?

Something he'd wanted to do from the moment he saw her in the emergency room last year. The day he'd discovered she was Wayne McKinna's daughter. And when he'd juggled his schedule to fly her to the islands.

This moment seemed predestined.

It would have been perfect if not for the flight that exposed the one thing he swore he'd never accept in a woman.

But that didn't stop him from licking his way across those luscious lips with tiny swipes of his tongue, his body flaming when her mouth opened, inviting him inside.

He slid home, the wet heat he found there setting off an explosion that burned away the line he'd drawn in the sand after his divorce—one he'd never cross if he was in his right mind.

But he wasn't, and he had no intention of retreating from this agonizing pleasure any time soon. The luscious friction against his tongue ratcheted up his need, hardening him beyond belief.

She made a tiny sound. Something that straddled the line between a complaint and a contented purr.

Her hands went to the back of his neck, pressing even closer.

Definitely not a complaint, then.

The sound came again.

Molly sucked down an audible breath and stiffened, causing Blake to freeze as well, his tongue still deeply embedded in her warmth.

He pieced together that the noise wasn't coming from her but from somewhere down…

She eased away, her lips sliding slowly over the length of

his tongue as they both withdrew. The separation was painful, not only for his mind, but for the area still pressed hard against her belly.

Ah, hell.

"The cat." The low huskiness of her voice scraped along nerve endings that were stretched to breaking point. He wanted nothing more than to lift her onto one of the kitchen counters and see if he could give that Scents of Pleasure sign outside a whole new meaning.

Her hands slid down to his shoulders and pushed slightly, her voice coming again. "The cat wants something."

To hell with the cat.

Then he smiled. Thoughts like that wouldn't endear him to her.

Neither would they solve the problem he was now facing.

He swallowed. What had he just allowed to happen? He was an even bigger idiot than he'd thought. He didn't want to fly her across the ocean, but he sure as hell would let himself get it on with her. And she'd just been out on a date with his best friend two days ago. The fact that Mark didn't play for keeps meant nothing at all.

Releasing her, he stepped back, hoping she wouldn't glance down for a couple of minutes.

Ha! Seeing as the cat was on the floor, there wasn't much chance of her not looking at it.

The floor, that was. Or noticing how she'd affected him in the process.

His eyes went to the source of the noise. Sure enough, the cat—body curved in a half-moon—had wrapped herself around one of Molly's legs. Its tail twitched back and forth as it craned its head up to look at her, the wide-eyed glance both innocent and cunning, the fur beneath its chin as white as newly fallen snow.

"Meooow."

The long drawn-out plea tugged at his heart, despite the lingering irritation at having his prize yanked from his grasp.

Molly gave him a shaky smile. "Well, she's definitely not feral, that's for sure."

The cat might not be, but he was starting to wonder about himself.

Since when had he allowed himself to be ruled by animal instinct?

How about every time he climbed in that cockpit to fly? Or whenever he got within ten feet of Molly McKinna.

How on earth was she able to gather her wits so quickly? He was still trying to figure out how to pull his knuckles off the floor and return to being a biped.

Crouching down, she held her hand out to the cat, who immediately slumped against it. Blake could hear the thing purr even from where he stood.

"What is it, sweetie? I know you have food." The cat trotted to the doorway of the other room, tail held high.

Since Molly was walking right beside her, there was no option but to follow them both. At least Molly's back was to him, giving him time to haul his body back into submission. A task none too easy since her rounded hips and the curve of her butt beckoned him closer.

Damn.

The cat glanced back at him and gave a haughty flick of her tail.

She knew exactly what she was doing. He'd seen his parents' pug do something similar whenever he'd gone to Florida to visit them. Jealously guarding its territory.

He doubted that plaintive little cry was anything other than a ploy to gain Molly's full attention. He'd use the same tactic if he thought it would work.

The animal went down the hallway and turned a corner, leaping onto the bed it found there.

Molly's bed.

He took a slow, careful breath as she reached out to the cat, her hand sliding over the animal's fur, her thumb stroking across its back, just like she'd done with his arm a few minutes ago. Blake tried not to remember the emotions that light touch had aroused in him, but it was impossible. Every second was permanently seared into his brain.

God, he wanted her. More than he should.

Forbidden fruit. The more dangerous it was, the more you craved it.

Eat it and you'll send yourself straight to some private hell.

He almost laughed. Not reaching out and plucking the apple from the tree was sending him to a hell of a different sort. Was one any better than the other?

Mark had set his sights on her, but was it because he genuinely liked her or because that was what Mark did? He saw, he conquered, he moved on to the next woman in line.

If Molly had a choice, who would she choose?

She'd just about kissed him into oblivion, which meant nothing in and of itself, but since he didn't see her as someone who batted her thick lashes at anyone she passed on the street…

He stopped himself right there.

Was he any better for her than Mark? He'd been so busy protecting himself that he'd never stopped to think about what was good for Molly. He'd warned her off his friend, but maybe he should have advised her to steer clear of him as well.

Could he see her without either of them getting hurt?

He didn't think so. The best thing to do would be to back off and give her some space. Let her get used to the island and to the work. See how she handled things without someone standing over her and pressuring her.

Could he do it? Could he leave her alone?

Hell, after that kiss, he wasn't sure. But he had to try. For both their sakes.

Even if it meant handing the winner's cup to his best friend.

CHAPTER ELEVEN

"WOULD you mind taking some EpiPens over to Akutan? Their clinic is out, and one of the volcano observatory guys has a bee allergy. He left his syringe in Anchorage." Sammi's voice came from the doorway. "I'd do it myself, but Screaming Jimmy is coming in at two."

Molly glanced up from the spider bite she'd been examining on a diabetic patient, a man in his early sixties. "Screaming Jimmy?"

Her patient exchanged a knowing smile with Sammi and said, "Believe me, you don't want to be here when he arrives. *I* don't want to be here…so if you could just give me a tube of antiseptic cream, I'll be on my way."

Okay, that still didn't answer her question. "Is he a kid?"

Sammi laughed. "Oh, he's all man—built like a tank. He just hates needles. He's coming in for a flu shot."

"Jimmy's an embarrassment to his gender," her patient grumbled.

"He literally screams?" Surely not.

"Like a banshee. He's the only guy I know who can shoot off a stream of cuss words all in falsetto." Sammi put two fingers against her open lips and swirled them away as if demonstrating. "He sounds kind of like a crazed opera singer."

Molly finished swabbing the infected bite with cream and

peeled apart a dressing to put over it. "Do you want me to administer the shot?"

"Oh, no. He won't let anyone else do it but me." She grimaced.

"Lucky girl." Molly scribbled a prescription on her pad and spoke to her patient. "Make sure you come back if this starts looking worse. And monitor your sugar."

The man gave a sheepish nod. "I will." He slid from the table. "That it?"

He was in a hurry, either because of Screaming Jimmy's impending visit or because he hadn't been careful about his sugar intake and wanted to avoid a lecture. Either way, she'd better follow up on him.

"Let's see you back next week, just to be sure." She handed him the prescription. "Call me if you have any problems before then."

Once he was gone, Sammi reached into a cabinet and pulled down five EpiPen boxes. "You okay with taking these?"

"Where's Akutan? Is it in one of the neighborhoods?"

"No, it's the next island over."

Molly's stomach pitched. "I have to fly there?"

Her reaction had nothing to do with fear this time, but everything to do with seeing Blake so soon after that disastrous kiss. Three days was definitely not enough time. Maybe a week. Two would be even better. Anything to give her a chance to regain her equilibrium and treat him like a colleague. A vague acquaintance. Especially after her date with Mark, which had been a huge disappointment.

She'd hoped to feel some of the same stirrings with him that she'd had with Blake. But Mark's chaste and polite kiss on the cheek at the door of her hotel room had been nothing compared to the knee-trembling reaction that had shot through her system the second Blake's lips had met hers. She sensed Mark had had the same lukewarm reaction, for which she was relieved.

It also meant she was in big trouble.

Sammi's voice brought her back to reality. "Only if you want to land on top of the volcano." The CHA grinned, straightening the band that held her thick braid in place. "The landing strip's not done yet. But they're working on it... Hey, I'm sure Blake wouldn't mind giving it a try, if you wanted him to..."

"No, that's okay." She could barely stomach landing on Dutch Harbor's runway, much less one that was still under construction. "So, if I don't fly, how exactly do I get there?"

"Boat. It's only about thirty-five miles away. There's a state ferry that travels between the islands every couple of weeks during the summer, but it's not due to dock for several days. The clinic has a boat we use for quick trips." She cocked her head. "You might as well look around while you're there. It's a nice little community. Only two or three cars in the whole place."

All Molly cared about was the word *boat*. That meant no flying. *Yes!* She wouldn't have to face Blake yet. As hard as she might try to stay cool and collected, she knew it was a lost cause. As soon as she saw him, it would all come rushing back. Every fantastic, horrifying second of it.

Had she lost her marbles?

Her experience with Gary should have taught her to keep her personal life and her professional life separate. At least in Anchorage, she and her ex had been in different wings of the hospital. And she had been careful to stick to the emergency room as much as possible.

Even after six months, though, the situation had been awkward, since he'd gone out of his way to run into her. And her mother hadn't helped matters, inviting the man over to dinner from time to time in the hope they might get back together.

The encounters had left her drained and exhausted. So much so that the Aleutians job had been a godsend—despite her fear of flying. And yet here she was, locking lips with the first man to cross her path. Worse, a pilot...and a colleague.

Maybe anyone looked good after what she'd left behind. And Blake seemed strong and capable but without the need to control everyone around him, like Gary. But how well did she really know him? He'd been through a painful breakup—he'd been married, for heaven's sake. Who knew what kind of baggage he carried around on those broad shoulders?

She had plenty of her own to lug around.

Getting involved with him was a catastrophe in the making. One she'd come here to avoid. She could and *would* remember that.

At all costs.

Sammi loaded the EpiPens in a little bag. "Just drop these off at the clinic in Akutan and they'll get one of them up to the observatory. Blake's going to meet you at the dock."

Her heart stuttered. "Blake? But I thought you said the airport—"

"I did. But when Blake's not doing medevacs or transporting patients to and from Anchorage, he works with the EMS department here on the island. I thought you knew that."

Emergency Medical Services. Great, that covered just about every job imaginable.

"No, I didn't." *All the more reason to keep your distance.* Yeah, that was going to be kind of hard if the guy did everything from driving ambulances to transporting pharmaceuticals between the islands.

"Here you go." Sammi handed her the bag of epinephrine syringes.

"I think I'd rather take my chances with Screaming Jimmy," she mumbled half under her breath on her way out the door.

Sammi evidently heard her, because she sent her off with a sustained upper-octave shriek—vibrato attached—that any opera singer would be proud to own.

Blake frowned as Molly's car pulled into the lot just as he was making sure the boat was topped up with fuel. He'd understood Sammi to say *she* was taking the medicine to the island, not Molly. If she was pulling a fast one, she was going to get an earful when he got back. He wasn't in the mood for matchmaking games. Not from anyone, even Sammi.

Huffing out a careful breath, he stood a little straighter. No big deal. They were both adults. One kiss was nothing. A fluke. People made mistakes and then moved on.

Just like he was going to do.

But seeing her get out of the car, thin blue sweater topping a casual pair of dark jeans, the raw, wild thrill that had accompanied the press of her lips to his—tongues sliding together—came rushing back. His brain wasn't the only body part that remembered.

He swore under his breath. The best he could hope for was to make this a quick trip. Zip over to Akutan, drop off the medicine, and hurry back to Unalaska. He'd be driving the boat the whole time.

"Sorry, I'm late."

"No problem." He took the bag from Molly and helped her onto the vessel, bracing himself when she brushed against him as she boarded. He released her hand and took a step back.

Keep it under control.

"Sorry." She gripped the chrome handrail that ran along the side as the boat rocked in time with the swells. "I tried to get Sammi to come, but she had a patient to deal with."

"You couldn't handle the patient?" He could have kicked himself the moment the words left his mouth when her face flushed the color of ripe strawberries. The slur was aimed at Sammi, but had hit Molly instead.

"She said she was the only one who could deal with this particular patient. H-he doesn't like shots, evidently."

Blake smiled, relief sweeping over him. Sammi hadn't been meddling, after all. "Jimmy?"

"Yes."

"Half of Jimmy's craziness is due to Sammi herself. He has a crush on her."

"Really? Does she know?"

"It's kind of obvious. Jimmy makes excuses to drop by the clinic every chance he gets. He's obnoxious enough that she has to deal with him personally."

Molly's fingers tightened on the rail, a frown appearing on her brow. "And she just puts up with it?"

"Jimmy's got a thick skull. Besides, he's ten years younger than Sammi, so she figures he'll eventually meet a girl he has more in common with and will leave her alone."

"Well, good luck to her. I hope she finds it easier than…"

He couldn't make out the last couple of words. "I'm sorry?"

"Nothing."

She seemed to be avoiding his glance. Who could blame her? The sooner they got to the island and back the better. "You ready?"

"Yep."

"Look on the bright side. The airport in Akutan is still under construction, so at least we're not flying in. Although we could probably borrow one of the amphibian planes, if you'd prefer."

"That's quite all right." She finally looked him in the eye with a smile as he turned the key to start the twin outboards. "Lucky for you, I'm not afraid of boats."

"Lucky for you, neither am I."

Her laughter floated on the air, the sound light and carefree, and a day that had been headed straight down suddenly began to look up.

It seemed to take less time than usual to arrive at Akutan. The wind had been chilly once they'd got away from the shelter of Dutch Harbor, so Molly had donned her coat and stayed in the cockpit area with him. Even in the enclosed space, the noise from the engines had made talking at anything less than a shout almost impossible, which was just as well. Blake had wanted to stick with the program this time. As long as he'd been busy manning a set of controls, he hadn't been able to do anything stupid. Besides, she seemed to have already put that kiss out of her mind.

If only he could do the same.

They arrived at the island and dropped the medicine off at the tiny clinic. Molly smiled at the wooden boardwalk system that linked different buildings to each other. "Sammi said there weren't very many cars—I can see why."

"There are a couple used for unloading supplies from the planes. And some of the folks have ATVs. As you can see, it's a pretty tiny place."

Sharon had come here with him once. What should have been a pleasant outing—and a chance to renew a troubled marriage—had turned into yet another war of words. *You actually have to walk everywhere?* They'd stayed a total of two hours, not even long enough to see the inside of the tiny inn, then they'd turned around and headed back to Unalaska. Two weeks later, Blake had returned from medevacing a critical patient and found Sharon had packed her bags and caught the ferry to Anchorage. She'd left a note. Tired and disheartened after losing the patient halfway through the flight, Blake hadn't gone after her. That had been the end. She'd filed for divorce soon afterward.

"Do you mind if I look around for a few minutes before we head back?"

He blinked. "Of course not."

A few minutes turned into a couple of hours and found them on the side of the mountain where salmonberry bushes twisted beside the steep footpath. She fingered one of the fuzzy leaves.

"A month ago, those would have been loaded with fruit," Blake said. "We can probably buy some jam made by the locals, if you want."

"That would be wonderful. Do they have these bushes in Unalaska as well?"

"Yep. They take vanloads of folks to pick them during season. It's one of the highlights of the year."

He waited for the scoffing he was so sure would come, but Molly just nodded, then turned to look out over the village and the bay down below. She slid out of her jacket and cinched it around her waist. "It's gorgeous here. The ocean seems to stretch forever."

There was a second or two in which he was afraid he wouldn't be able to answer her, and he had to swallow the lump that formed in his throat. "You're lucky it's a clear day. You normally can't see this well."

"I'm very lucky." She raked both hands through her hair and set it loose again, the strands catching the light as they settled back into place. "I feel free."

Said as if it were something she hadn't been for a very long time. Was that how Sharon had felt when she'd fled their marriage?

Hell. This was something he needed to back away from right now.

"Are you ready? We can pick up that jelly on the way to the boat."

A flicker of something that might have been disappointment went through her eyes. "Sorry, Blake. You probably have plenty of other things to do, and I should get back and see how Sammi fared with Jimmy."

He did have plenty to do, not the least of which was scrubbing the sight of Molly standing on the side of the mountain from his memory. Along with the sudden need to lay her down on the rocky path and kiss her senseless.

Damn.

Time to be proactive.

He started down the path, hoping that if he could move fast enough, he could outrun the longing that threatened to sweep through him.

But even as they boarded the boat for the return trip and Blake throttled up the engines to skim across the water and away from the island, the uneasy sensation followed him, refusing to be left behind no matter how fast he went.

All he could hope was that the two jars of salmonberry jam he'd purchased were the only souvenirs he'd have from this particular trip.

But even as he thought it, a little piece of his heart was already shrugging off that idea as a pipe dream. Because Molly had gotten inside his head. And despite his best efforts, she wasn't going anywhere.

CHAPTER TWELVE

THE champagne fizzed as it hit her skin, icy bubbles bursting as the liquid waterfall cascaded over her collarbone, rushing downward to squeeze through the valley between her breasts. She arched her back, a moan hovering on her lips.

Blake!

Goose bumps formed on her arms, but the chill didn't last long. Warm lips chased after the river, tongue flicking to capture each drop of alcohol before it could escape. She laughed as his mouth came up to meet hers, a dinner bell going off somewhere in the distance.

No food. Not now.

Blake ignored the sound, kissing her long and deep, the taste of the expensive beverage mingling with that of her own skin, the bell going off again. A frown formed on her brow.

Leave us alone!

He raised his head and looked down at her, pupils wide and dark with…

The bell grew more persistent now. Coming closer. Next to her ear.

Her eyes popped open and Blake slid away, disappearing into the shadows. Gasping, she tried to place where she was, who the warm body against her side belonged to. What that sound was.

Bed. Cat. Phone. The words presented themselves, and reality intruded. Molly sat up with a groan.

Lordy, that had been…

Unthinkable!

She grabbed her cellphone from the side table. "Hello?"

"Molly." Blake's voice came over the line, the low growl nothing like the one from her dreams. It was so tempting to just fade away, to feel the… "Molly! Are you there?"

She grabbed a quick breath, trying to banish Dream Blake and replace him with reality. "Yes. I'm here."

"We need you down at the clinic. Now. One of the fishing boats just came in with a crewman with a possible head injury."

The last vestiges of sleep deserted her as she crawled from beneath the covers, trying to avoid the cat, who'd lifted her head to glare at Molly in the dark. "I'll be right there."

She dragged a hanger from the closet which was already loaded with a complete outfit, a habit ingrained from her thirty-hour shifts as an intern—when she could barely think, much less put together a matching set of clothes. Not bothering with the light, she threw her sweats onto the bed in a heap and dressed in the clean clothing.

Head injury. That meant an automatic trip to Anchorage, no questions asked.

Grabbing her keys and coat, she prayed she'd left enough dry food in Samita's—the cat's new name a joke between her and Sammi—bowl to hold her over until she got back. She'd call Sammi, who had a set of keys to Molly's house, and ask her to check later.

She arrived at the clinic in fifteen minutes flat and found the front doors opened. Blake was just inside with Sammi, the patient already on a stretcher, an emergency services vehicle idling out front.

"Condition?" she asked as she hurried forward.

"Pulse is strong. I've just started an IV…" Sammi looked up "…but his left pupil is blown. A crab pot hit him in the temple."

God.

"Name and age?"

"Peter Laughlin, age nineteen."

So young.

Molly knew from treating other commercial fishermen that empty crab pots were heavy, close to eight hundred pounds each. And in rough seas with fully loaded pots, things turned dangerous really quickly. She glanced at Blake, nothing going through her mind except getting off the ground as fast as possible. "Let's go."

They raced to the airport, getting there within five minutes. Blake had already called ahead, so the plane was standing by, all other air traffic halted until they could get off the ground. While she worked in the back, hooking the patient up to the heart monitor, Blake got them into the air as fast as possible. Molly braced herself during takeoff, no time to worry about anything but her patient. Once airborne, she rerecorded his vitals, relaying every bit of information she could to Alaska Regional. The on-call neurosurgeon had already been contacted and would meet them at the hospital. She glanced at her watch. Three a.m. They should arrive by six.

"Hang in there, Peter," she whispered, squeezing the young man's hand.

A thought crossed her mind. "Blake," she called over the sound of the engines, "has anyone contacted his family?"

"Sammi's working on it now. Mark can fly them in if they're on one of the islands. I've already called him, he's ready to move."

He had? She wondered if Blake had mentioned their kiss.

Neither the time nor place, Molly.

The aircraft bumped a couple of times, but she stayed in

place, her eyes never leaving her patient. "No construction zones today, please."

So many things could go wrong with head injuries—brain bleeds, swelling, pressure that grew to a point that brain cells died.

Molly continued to monitor him throughout the flight, checking Peter's ears and nose for any sign of drainage, which would mean an increase in pressure. Still nothing, so at least brain fluid wasn't leaking from the skull cavity. But that blown pupil worried her. And over the past hour he'd developed telltale signs of raccoon eyes—both orbits turning a deep purple—which pointed to skull fracture, probably at his temple, which was also discolored and swollen.

After what seemed like an eternity Blake said, "We're descending, Molly. Get him ready for transport."

Thank God. "Does the hospital have everything in place?"

"They'll meet us outside. The surgeon is standing by."

Molly had done everything she could. It was time to pass the torch to the next group of caregivers who would work to save the young man's life.

Within fifteen minutes the wheels of the aircraft touched down.

Just another minute or two, Peter.

The plane slowed dramatically, and Molly made sure the patient and the IV bags stayed secure.

"Taxiing over to the hospital area now."

Each tiny bump in the runway seemed magnified as she waited for them to arrive. She took the patient's hand in hers and spoke softly, not knowing whether or not he could hear her but doing anything she could think of to reach inside him and urge him to keep fighting.

The plane pulled to a stop, the propellers slowing down. Blake was at her side in less than a minute, unlocking the wheels to the stretcher and getting the side door open. A group of hospital staff was already waiting outside. Once the patient was on the ground, she ran beside the group, giving them an update and handing over her case notes. Inside the doors they raced down the hallway, one of the emergency room doctors—someone she didn't recognize—glancing at her. "We'll take it from here."

She blinked, still running, before she realized he was telling her not to come any farther. Stopping in her tracks, she watched the stretcher pull out of view, the doctor communicating with the surgeon as he went. "He wants a CAT scan, STAT."

Then they were gone, and the world rushed back into focus. What had been fast-forward action slowed to a crawl. Molly stood in the middle of the hospital hallway, at a loss, her heart still pounding with the rush of adrenaline but with nothing to expend it on any more. This was different from Jed's injury, which hadn't been as serious. She clasped her hands in front of her, trying to figure out what to do. She was used to finishing one case and immediately starting in on the next. And the next.

This was strange. Wrong. There was nothing for her to focus on. Nothing to…

A light touch on the shoulder made her jump. She whirled around.

Blake.

She pulled in a deep breath, her legs shaking. "What do I do?" The whispered words came from somewhere deep inside.

He squeezed her shoulder. "We go and get some coffee. Come on."

Molly was used to calling the shots, but at the moment she was out of her element, very glad to have someone else to lean on, if only for a few minutes. He didn't take her to the break room but to the deserted cafeteria, which she appreciated. It wasn't open for breakfast yet, but the coffee machine was there.

"How do you like it?" he asked.

"Cream. No sugar."

Blake fixed hers first and went to a nearby table. "Sit. I'll be right back."

She lowered herself into the chair and started shivering. The temperature on the plane had been icy, but she hadn't noticed it until now. Wrapping her hands around her coffee, she tried to absorb the heat into her system.

Blake's coffee was black. Dark. He moved his chair next to hers. "You okay?"

"Wh-why is your plane so damn c-cold?" To her horror, her teeth were chattering.

"You left your coat at the clinic." He wrapped his arm around her and pulled her close, the warmth of his body hitting her. "And handing our patients over to someone else takes some getting used to."

"I've worked in an emergency room for two years. I should already be used to it."

"How did you unwind after shifts?"

She attempted a smile. "I went to bed."

"This is a different world. You go from nothing to a hundred miles an hour in a few seconds, then back down to nothing just as fast. Your body will adjust."

"Did yours?"

He nodded. "I've been doing this for a long time."

She laid her head on Blake's shoulder, knowing it wasn't a smart move, but the continued warmth from his body made her aware she'd only had a little bit of sleep last night. "Sorry. I don't know what's wrong with me." She yawned. "Maybe I'll store an extra coat on the plane."

"Probably not a bad idea." His arm tightened. "Why don't you close your eyes for a few minutes?"

"I should go to my mother's house and get some sleep."
She paused. Her mom's was the last place she wanted to go.
But Blake had to be exhausted as well. "Do you have anyone
you can stay with?"

He didn't answer for a minute, then said, "Not any more."

Before she had a chance to process his words, Doug appeared around the corner, skidding to a stop in front of them.

Molly lifted her head when her friend's brows went up. "I
didn't expect to see you here so early."

"It's almost seven. Time for the next shift. I heard you'd
brought a patient in." He gave her a pointed look. "And so
has Gary. He's on his way."

CHAPTER THIRTEEN

GARY BRANDON, bigshot cardiologist. Well-traveled speaker.
Molly's ex.

Someone Blake would rather not see.

As if on a cord, Molly pushed her chair away from Blake's,
the shriek of metal against tile echoing off the walls around
them. "Do you mind if we leave? I don't care where we go."

The man who'd warned Molly moved in and squeezed
her arm. "I'll try to hold him off for a minute, if you want."

"Thanks, Doug. I'd appreciate it."

Blake got to his feet, not exactly sure what was going on,
but Molly obviously didn't want to run into the guy. Why that
should make his psyche do a quick slide across the floor he
had no idea. "We can go back to the plane. I'm okay to fly,
if you want to go home."

Home. Unalaska wasn't Molly's home. At least not yet. But
the word had sounded good coming off his tongue.

"Yes. Thanks." She gave her friend a quick hug. "I owe
you."

He lifted his brows. "Bet you're glad I made you get on
that flight now."

"Get out of here." Molly rolled her eyes, then turned and
headed for the nearest exit. "Is the plane still in front of the
hospital?"

"They've probably already moved it to the hangar. We can

get there through here." He shrugged out of his coat and put it around her shoulders as they made their way to the door.

Molly shoved her arms through the sleeves. "This is getting to be a habit."

One that was going to be hard for him to break.

Sure enough, the plane was no longer on the stretch of tarmac behind the hospital, so they walked toward the terminal. It was chilly outside, but Blake was used to the weather. Besides, he needed to clear his head. Not wanting to see her ex meant nothing. He'd bet Sharon had no desire to run into him any time soon either. Maybe *he* was simply the lesser of two evils in Molly's mind.

"You won't say anything, about my trying to avoid him, will you? I'd rather he not know."

"Gary was the man you dated?" He already knew the answer, but her reaction to Doug's news made him uneasy.

Molly glanced at him. "I guess the hospital grapevine is alive and well."

He nodded, preferring not to tell her he'd seen them together at the hospital or the irritation he'd felt while standing in line at the cafeteria and hearing the man cut Molly off in midsentence when she'd tried to make a point about hospital policy. He might be charming and good at what he did, but the guy was an overbearing jerk. Or was that just his own reaction to seeing Molly with him?

"Anyway," she went on, "things were…awkward at the end."

Realization dawned. "That's why you took the job at the clinic."

"Yes." She paused. "And I'd rather that didn't get out either."

"I told you, I can keep a secret."

She shot him another glance and gave a quick laugh.

"You've said that before. You're not with the CIA or any-thing, right?"

"Not CIA, but I was in the service. Navy."

They reached the hangar, only to find the plane was in the process of being refueled. He opened the door so they'd at least have some shelter from the wind.

"Were you a pilot there as well?"

"Yep."

"Really?" She smiled. "I didn't know the navy recruited stunt pilots."

He didn't return her smile. Just like Molly had wanted to avoid her ex, this was one subject he'd rather steer clear of. So why had he mentioned being in the navy in the first place? Maybe because he wanted to gauge her reaction. He sucked down a deep breath and went for it. "I was a fighter pilot."

A fighter pilot.

Molly's throat tightened. What had started as light teas-ing on her part turned deadly serious. If he'd wanted an Evel Knievel-style job, a combat pilot was about as close as one could get. So what was he doing, flying shuttle service from Alaska to the Aleutians? "Why'd you get out?"

He paused and leaned against one of the hangar walls. "Just decided it wasn't where I needed to be."

That was a nonanswer if she ever heard one. Time to drop the lid on the curiosity box and lock it tight. If he wanted to tell her more, he would.

Move to a safer subject.

Before she could think of one, he jammed his hands in his pockets and looked away from her. "On the way home from a training mission, a buddy of mine had some trouble with his aircraft. We made it back to the carrier and thought we were home free." Blake stopped for a second. "His timing was off—whether it was due to engine malfunction or pilot error, I'm not sure. Anyway, he overshot the flight deck and his hook missed the wires completely. In trying to pull up to come back around… He didn't make it."

Molly understood almost nothing of what he'd described, but the raw grief in his voice told her everything she needed to know. Blake's friend had died during a flight. Just like her father had. Her heart ached. "I'm sorry."

"It was a long time ago."

"Even so." She wanted to touch him, but his crossed arms and tight jaw warned her not to. "That's why you got out?"

"That and…" he gave a hard laugh "…after the accident, my wife threatened to divorce me if I stayed in after my six years were up."

"Oh." He'd done as his ex-wife had asked, so he must have saved the marriage. At least temporarily. But in the end it hadn't been enough. Who'd initiated that final separation?

None of your business, Molly. Remember that lid you just closed? Keep it shut.

Why would a woman divorce a man like this? What wasn't to like about him?

That flash of straight white teeth and accompanying dimple when he laughed—even in anger—had gone right to her stomach, wiping her mind clear of any rational thought. The long sexy groove in his cheek was like an open invitation, and her eyes wanted nothing more than to stick around and explore further.

The words came out before she could stop them. "Your wife was a fool."

Their eyes met and held. Molly wrapped her arms around her waist, her mouth going dry. Why had she said that?

She'd never felt this unsteady around a man. Not even Gary.

Fear of flying. It had thrown everything out of whack. Including her emotions.

It made sense. She'd met Blake and almost immediately

had received a shot of adrenaline large enough to bring down an elephant. Put her nerves on edge enough times, and her reactions to him were bound to become ingrained, just like Pavlov's dog.

Ding, ding, ding. She could almost hear the little bell that had sent the poor dog's salivary glands into a frenzy.

At least she didn't drool.

Yet.

A man peeked inside the hangar door. "Plane's fueled up and ready to go."

Blake straightened, his gaze slipping away. "Thanks."

Once on the plane, he checked switches and buttons, a dizzying combination she couldn't even begin to grasp. He'd said she could fly if she had to. She didn't see how. Nothing on that panel made any sense to her.

"Buckle in." His voice had gone back to pilot mode—not that the pitch was any lower than it was on the ground. He just infused it with a dose of calm certainty that said all would be well.

Yeah. And her nervous system still wasn't buying it. Not yet, anyway. Fastening her seat belt, she pulled in a deep breath. "You sure you're not too tired to fly back?"

"I'm fine." He glanced to the side. "Do you need to take something?"

"I'll be okay." Sure she would.

All too soon they were speeding down the runway, then into the air. To her surprise, her stomach tagged along for the ride this time. *Yay.* That was a step in the right direction.

"You're clutching again."

"What?"

"Hands."

She glanced down and blew her breath out in frustration. "Sorry." She released her grip.

"I really am a decent pilot."

His tone held not a hint of boasting. He wanted to reassure her. Nothing more.

"I know." She held her arms out straight and wiggled her fingers. "Look…no hands."

He sat up, rolling his shoulders as if relieving an ache. "Do that while landing, and I'll be suitably impressed."

"I bet I can." *Gulp. What?*

But it worked. As they swooped down toward Dutch Harbor with its minuscule landing strip three hours later, she pressed herself deep into her seat, but held her hands up dutifully. They shook harder than the plane had during that first storm, but she kept them where they were. She did close her eyes, however.

They touched down—the lightest of bumps telling her they'd made it back to the island. Still alive. She parted her lids as Blake taxied off the runway, following the guidance of the ground crew. Once there, the engines shut down with a sigh of relief.

"Wow! Did you see that? I did it! No hands." No one was more surprised than she was.

"You certainly did."

He unstrapped his harness and shoved it away before turning toward her. The flare of heat in his gaze made her breath catch in her throat. Her lips parted.

Had she done something wrong?

Without a word he curved his hand around the back of her neck and hauled her toward him. She barely had time to gasp in a desperate bid to get some air into her lungs before his mouth came down hard on hers.

CHAPTER FOURTEEN

MOLLY gripped his shoulders, frowning when her buckle held her in place, not allowing her to get closer.

Suddenly the strap gave away. Had he undone it?

She didn't care. Her arms went around his neck as his lips continued to move over hers, the hard initial kiss softening into something closer to coaxing.

No need. She was already there. So there.

Fingers delved into her hair and cupped her head, tilting her face to the side just a bit, allowing him to deepen the kiss.

From somewhere within her a moan rose to the surface—just like in her dream earlier. Blake broke contact to look into her eyes. Evidently okay with what he saw, he dipped in for another kiss.

A tattoo rapped against the side of the plane, stopping him. "Damn."

They both looked toward the sound and saw a couple members of the small airport's ground crew grinning up at them, one backing up with a wrench he'd evidently used to tap on the plane. He made some kind of signal.

Blake swore softly again, his breathing as ragged as hers was. The hand in her hair slid away, and he gave the crew a thumbs-up sign. "They need to secure the plane so they can move on to the next one coming in."

"Oh."

Molly quickly cleaned up the medical area in back, while Blake shut down the controls. They then walked toward the parking lot in relative silence. But the feeling of his lips on hers thrummed through her, refusing to let up no matter how hard she tried to shift her mind to other things. And the look in his eyes…

She shuddered, digging in her purse for her keys, gripping them tightly once she found them. Only her car wasn't here. It was still at the clinic.

"You okay?" He'd come up behind her.

Please don't let that be regret in his voice.

She turned to face him, wishing she had something to lean against for support. "Not really. You?"

He bent close, his warm breath brushing her ear as he murmured, "No. Definitely not. My plane isn't the place I would have chosen for any of this to happen."

Her heart leapt. He had a preferred venue? And just where was that?

"No?"

He brushed a lock of hair behind her ear. "I'm not sure what's going on between us, but am I mistaken in thinking that kiss wasn't completely one-sided?"

A soft laugh broke free. "You aren't mistaken."

Searching her eyes, he said, "I'm trying to do the right thing here, Molly, but I'm having a hell of a time."

"The right thing being?"

"Taking you back to the clinic and letting you drive away."

She swallowed hard, the chill of the air seeping through Blake's coat. "Is that what you want?"

"I don't know what I want."

"Would it help if I said I didn't want to drive away? If I asked you to take me back to your place instead of the clinic?"

Did you just proposition the man? Heat washed over her face.

He went very still. "If we go back there, it won't be to sleep."

"I know."

"And you still want to?"

She nodded, afraid to let her tongue loose again. Who knew what it might come up with next?

He took her keys from her hand and pocketed them as if afraid she might change her mind and make a run for it. How? Her car was nowhere around.

"You can take me to pick up my car later this morning."

"I don't think so." He took her hand and backed her toward his own car. "If you come home with me, you're mine until this afternoon. No one expects us back before then."

The sensual promise behind those words kicked her heart into gear, just like when he throttled up the engines of the plane as he prepared to take off. She should be afraid of the dark gleam in his eyes. But she wasn't. She felt nothing but elation. Wonder. The gorgeous pilot who'd taken none of the women from the hospital to bed was taking her home with him.

Thinking about the "whys" would do her no good. Better to just sit back and enjoy their time together, no matter how brief. They reached the passenger door of his red Mustang. He didn't open it, evidently waiting for a response to his declaration.

"Okay. This afternoon, then." She hesitated. "I do need to show up at the clinic after that."

"I know." A slight frown appeared between his brows before the muscles released, and he opened the door, allowing her to slide inside.

He went around to his side of the car and climbed in, slamming the door behind him. He gripped the steering wheel for a moment before shoving the keys into the ignition. She waited for him to turn the engine over, but he just sat there.

Second thoughts? "Are you sure you want to do this?"

"Yes." He swiveled toward her and brushed his knuckles across her cheek. "Just trying to remember something."

She was pretty sure he wasn't trying to remember how to actually *do* it. It had to be like riding a bike. Once you took the training wheels off, you never forgot how to pedal. Ever. Especially someone like him.

Leaning over, he closed in for a brief kiss. "I don't think I have anything at the house."

"Anything?" The last thing she wanted to think about was eating. "If you're talking about food, I'm not really hungry."

A low chuckle broke free. "Not food. Definitely not food. But I do need to stop at the store."

"Oh." She realized what he meant. *"Oh!"*

His fingers drifted down her cheek to her throat, pausing at the spot where her pulse was beating up a storm. "I wish I didn't live so damned far away."

"Is anything far on this island?"

She understood what he meant, though. She wanted his lips back on hers. Didn't want to stop at any stupid drug store, but for once she wasn't being the sensible one. Ever since she'd agreed to take this job, it seemed her ability to stop and make rational decisions had been tossed into the nearest medical waste receptacle. But taking her hands off the seat of that plane and holding them up for him to see had given her a rush like none she'd ever felt. Was this what her father had experienced on every flight? If so, she could understand his fascination with his job.

His fingers curved around her nape like they had on the plane, his thumb still strumming the side of her throat. The heat his touch generated had nothing to do with the cool fall temperatures and everything to do with warming her from within. She could barely believe she'd soon be burrowing deep under the covers with this man.

Hurry!

Maybe something in her eyes gave her away, because he leaned in for another soft kiss before starting the car and backing out of the parking space. Once headed away from the airport, he located a store in short order. "I'll be right back."

"Okay."

Was she doing the right thing here? She'd been dead set against getting involved with another colleague. Almost seeing Gary at the hospital should have knocked some sense into her.

On the other hand, by spending this time with Blake, maybe she could funnel away some of the growing tension between them and life could return to normal. She could look on it as a quick fling—plenty of her peers indulged in brief affairs after all. Otherwise, if she took this too seriously and something went wrong—she bit her lip—things could get ugly really fast.

Blake was back within five minutes, toting a small plastic bag. See-through. Heavens. Nothing like advertising what they were about to do to the world. The whole island would probably know in short order.

He climbed inside and tossed the bag into the backseat. "Do you want to take a nap?"

"Can't."

Switching the heater vents on, he pulled out of the lot. "I hope there's a good reason for that."

"Definitely." Against her better judgment, she gave voice to something she'd thought of earlier. "You never considered dating anyone at the hospital?"

"No."

A one-word answer. Okay, so this was something he wasn't anxious to discuss. And he was obviously smarter than she was in that regard.

What did it matter? Neither of them was looking for anything permanent.

He surprised her by expanding on his answer. "As you've guessed, my marriage wasn't exactly a happy one once I took this job."

She took a second to digest his words. He'd said his wife had threatened to divorce him if he didn't stop flying fighter jets. He'd done as she asked, and she still hadn't been happy? "She didn't want you to fly at all?"

"Oh, she was fine with my flying. Just not as a military pilot. And certainly not as a bush pilot. And she wanted nothing to do with Unalaska. She wanted to me to change over to commercial passenger jets. Go back to living in Anchorage, or move to another—bigger—city. I tried, but I hated it. And she hated that I hated it." His jaw tightened. "Sorry. I don't know why I brought that up."

A subtle warning, maybe? A declaration that he'd choose his job over any relationship?

"My fault. I asked about your personal life." She was going to ruin everything, if she wasn't careful. "Can we rewind?"

He paused. "To how far back?"

"To before." Maybe he'd changed his mind after all? "Do you still want to go through with this?"

"Do you?"

She blinked at him. "Yes. Definitely."

His slow smile drew her to him, along with that damned crease in his cheek. "Good answer."

"It *was* good, wasn't it?" She forced some bravado into her voice. Actually, the courage came from knowing he still wanted her.

His hand slid over hers. "Yes, but it's about to get a whole lot better."

* * *

First the silky scarf around her neck, then those small pink buttons on the sweater that lay just beneath the jacket. One button at a time.

Maybe it wasn't the coolest move to plan exactly which pieces of clothing would be the first to go, but the pressure was building. Not just behind his zipper but in his head and in his chest. He wasn't sure if it was pleasure or desperation. Maybe a mixture of the two.

A wave of need had washed over him as soon as she'd unclenched her hands from the seat. Yes, she'd been scared, but that fear had changed to elation once they'd landed. He'd seen it in her face. And there'd been no hint that she wanted to stay in Anchorage. In fact, she'd been anxious to get back to the island. Yes, it had been because of her ex, but he sensed she liked it here.

He drove the streets by rote, clicking his blinker on and off at the appropriate times. When he finally reached his driveway, he pulled into it, seeing the place through critical eyes as he shut off the engine. Unimaginative white paint coated everything in sight. Empty flower beds. Lawn in need of a good cut.

He hadn't taken very good care of his parents' home.

Because it wasn't a home. Not any more. It was a place to sleep and not much else. The last woman he'd brought here had been his wife.

No one else. Until Molly.

He swallowed. It didn't mean anything. His career kept him busy.

"Aren't you going to invite me in?" Molly's low voice came from beside him, a hint of uncertainty coloring the words.

Damn.

"Yeah, I was just noticing what sorry shape the place is in."

"It's fine, Blake." She hesitated. "Or would you rather go back to my place?"

"Too far away." Leaning across the seat, he kissed her, preferring actions to pretty words. He'd learned during his marriage that he didn't always know what to say to a woman.

And she tasted wonderful. This was so much better than talking anyway. He raised his head. "Ready to go in?"

Her tongue scooped across her lower lip. "In a minute. After you do that again."

"Gladly." He smiled and drew her close, the heady feel of her open mouth calling him home. Unable to resist, he slid inside, taking time to explore the textures and softness he found there. His body responded, knowing that as good as this felt—and damn if it didn't feel good—there were other things that were going to set his furnace burning on high. So many things he wanted to do to her...for her.

Molly's fingers slid into his hair, her thumbs following the shape of his ears and stroking along them. His whole scalp turned warm. That heat traveling down his jaw and centering on their joined mouths. Her tongue slid along his, the exact way he imagined her bare calf would float along the back of his thigh as he entered her. Slowly, drawing out each ounce of sensation.

He needed to get her into the house, but he couldn't seem to move from this spot. Couldn't stop kissing her.

Who needed to breathe? All he wanted—needed—was this woman and the crazy mix of emotions she pulled from him.

The sound of a car slowly traveling down the street made him pull back.

Neighborhood watch.

The two elderly gentlemen heading up the program wouldn't hesitate to stop and put their hands to the sides of his tinted windows to see what was going on inside the vehicle. The last thing he wanted was for them to find him making out with the island's new doctor.

He glanced at her, taking in her flushed cheeks, the plump red lips that looked totally ravished. "Let's go inside."

"Okay."

Oh, yeah. That husky word sent any number of sensual thoughts roaring through his skull.

He opened his door and got out, moving around to open Molly's door. He found her reaching into the backseat, straining to get something.

Of course, the condom package. He'd completely forgotten. Not good.

She exited with the plastic bag and handed it to him with a sly smile. Being a doctor, protection was probably something she stressed time and time again to her patients. He should be glad she was so careful, but at the moment he felt clumsy and unsure.

How long had it been again?

Too long.

He glanced at the street, but the car had disappeared. No way of telling if it really had been the neighborhood patrol guys or not. But he didn't want to wait around for them to come cruising back, in case it had been.

Molly wrapped her hands around his arm and snuggled close as he flipped his key ring around his index finger until it landed on his house key. "If a car drives by, don't make eye contact with whoever's inside."

"What?"

He rolled his eyes. Why had he said that? "I have some nosy neighbors."

"Is it a problem that I'm here?"

This was why he should stick to kissing and leave the talking to men who did it better than he did. Like Mark.

His jaw tightened. Molly was here with *him*, not with Mark. "No, it's not a problem. They'll just talk your ear off if you let them." He pulled her closer. "And talking's the last thing I want to do right now."

And that, my dear Sherlock, was the truth.

As soon as they walked through the door, he threw the keys and the little bag on the table in the entryway and drew her against him. "Do you want something to drink?"

"No."

"Eat?"

"It depends. Is it something interesting?" She sent him another knowing smile that had his mind off and running in all directions.

Exactly how did you answer a question like that? "Depends on what you find interesting."

"You."

"That's what I was hoping you'd say."

Blake's mouth was on hers in an instant, all the hunger he'd shoved to the side washing over him in a flood that threatened to swamp his senses. Her hands gripped his shirt, whether to pull him closer or to keep from being shoved backward by the force of his kiss, he had no idea. But whatever the reason, he liked it. Liked that she seemed just as eager for him as he was for her.

With one hand on the small of her back and the other cupping her head, he eased her backward step by step, never taking his lips from hers.

How many times had he come home late at night so exhausted he'd found his way to the bedroom in the dark? Lots. He could do this with both hands tied behind his back. Or better yet, with Molly's hands tied behind her back.

Before they'd covered five steps, she tugged her mouth from his, bringing a frown to his face. "Bag," she muttered.

"Your purse?" *Stop talking and keep kissing, woman.*

"Condoms."

"Right." He let go of her for the two seconds it took him

to cross the hall and retrieve the bag. That was the second time he'd almost forgotten them and the second time she'd remembered. Was he really that messed up over the thought of having her at last?

Oh, yeah.

Condom package in hand, he moved toward her, only to find she was already in the living room, her head tilted as she studied something on the wall. Reaching up, she touched a framed snapshot, her head swiveling toward him. The question was there in her eyes, even before her mouth formed the words.

"Blake, where did you get this?"

CHAPTER FIFTEEN

"Your father gave it to me."

Molly's breathing thickened as she stared at the picture of her dad beside an airplane very much like the one Blake now piloted. A smile wreathed his face, while one hand rested on the aircraft beside him. She could almost imagine him caressing the metal framework in pride. She hadn't seen her father this happy in a long time. "When was it taken?"

"Does it matter?" He moved to stand beside her, draping one arm around her waist, making no move to take up where they'd left off.

Her fingers touched the face in the photograph, remembering patting it as a child. He'd smiled back then, too. Big beaming smiles that had made her heart swell with love. "He looks happy."

"Yes."

"Did you take the picture?"

He nodded. "I had it framed for his birthday." He paused, a muscle working in his jaw. "He gave it back to me a couple of weeks before his plane went down. Said it was a graduation present for completing my training."

His fingers tightened on her waist. "He was a good friend."

"I'm glad." Her brain struggled to work through seeing her father through someone else's lens. "I miss him."

"I know."

She believed he really did know. "I never really saw this part of my dad's life. My mom tried to protect me. Probably too much. She ended up resenting my father for keeping his job; she said it meant more to him than we did. She always badgered him to…" a sudden thought came to her "…quit. To become a commercial pilot. Like your wife wanted you to be. That's strange. Did you guys ever talk about it? Did you know about my mom?"

The arm behind her back stiffened. "We talked about a lot of things."

They had talked about it. Something about that hurt. Like a stranger peering into her bedroom window and seeing all her secrets.

Well, Blake hadn't been a stranger to her dad, but he'd been an unknown to her at the time.

"I see."

Blake turned her to face her. "He loved you very much, Molly. He was so proud of your accomplishments, that you were making great grades in med school."

Her vision went misty, and she blinked a couple of times. Blake came back into view.

Strong. Stable.

A man her father had been able to count on as a confidant. Someone with whom he had shared his deepest, darkest secrets, and never worried about them getting out. The way Blake had promised to keep hers.

In that moment, her heart expanded with an emotion she couldn't quite identify. An amalgamation of grief, wonder, and something else. Something she refused to put a name to. Instead, she took Blake's hands, the plastic bag he held crackling as she did.

"Take me to bed."

His Adam's apple dipped as he stared into her face. "You sure?"

"Never more sure of anything in my life."

Before she could say another word, he scooped her into his arms and carried her down the hall—her father's picture receding from her sight, his bright smile burned into her memory. She snuggled closer, lifting her head to plant several kisses along the underside of Blake's jaw. She wanted this man. A man her father had cared about. Maybe it was one more step toward finding peace with his memory.

That was what that wave of emotion had been about. It had to be.

Would Blake care that she was using him to exorcize this particular demon?

No, because he was using her to gain a little satisfaction of his own, so they could call it even, after tonight.

They entered a darkened room. She couldn't see, but Blake moved surely toward the center of the space and set her down. Her back met the softness of a coverlet and she sank into the welcoming warmth.

"Lights on or off?" He leaned down to kiss her, smoothing her hair away from her face as he did.

"Don't leave me." The words had nothing to do with the lights, and everything to do with being as close to this man as she could get.

"I won't." He settled next to her, resting on his elbow. All she could see was the glittering of his eyes as he looked down at her.

"Kiss me." She wanted to lose herself in him. Or was it to find herself? Everything inside her twisted and turned, nothing seeming to make sense any more.

Nothing.

Except Blake.

He did as she asked, kissing her softly. Too softly. She wanted more. Asked for it, her tongue sliding along the seam of his lips and pushing inside.

A groan rose from his throat as she delved deeper. The sound intoxicated her, made her think of all the ways she could make him growl with pleasure. She wanted to do each and every one of them before the night was over. And more. So much more.

Needing to keep him close, she reached up to hold him in place, the warm texture of his neck drawing her attention. She tested it, the tiny hairs at his nape tickling her fingertips.

While she explored the small amount of exposed skin, Blake curved a hand around her rib cage, the splayed fingertips spanning half her width.

Big. Everything about him was solid, making her feel… what? Weak.

No, not weak.

Cherished. That was it.

Her hands moved down his back, bunching his shirt and tugging it from his waistband. More skin. Warm. Inviting. Her half-closed lids melted against each other, fusing shut.

That silky first touch of skin deceived, though. Because beneath that softness lay ridges of muscle that were firm. Strong. She pressed her fingertips against them experimentally.

He raised his head to look at her. "You okay?"

"Yes. Except for this." She tugged harder on his shirt, using her actions to ask him for help.

In a second he'd shrugged out of it, casting it to the side.

She sat up as well, running her fingers over his chest, the lightest smattering of crisp hair meeting her touch. It was too dark to see the color, but she imagined it dark brown. She followed the trail down, loving the way his abs shuddered beneath her hands as she slowly skimmed over them. The band of hair narrowed below his belly button where the waistband of his trousers halted her progress. But not for long.

"Wait." The graveled command stopped her in her tracks.

Surely he wasn't about to back out. Was he?

Oh, please. Don't.

"I'm not sure I unders—"

"It's..." He cupped her face and kissed her. "It's been a long time."

She saw. Smiled. "It's okay. It's been a while for me, too."

As if she'd just released a spring that had been holding him back, his next kiss was anything but tender. Devouring her in the way she'd craved from the moment he'd carried her through that doorway.

Her shirt came off, his fingers tracing down her spine until he came to the catch on her bra. Hardly slowing him down, he unlatched it as he continued on his way. His tongue pushed into her mouth, sending a shot of heat rushing down her stomach and pooling between her legs. She shifted closer, wishing she'd remained on the bed instead of sitting up. Body parts didn't match up this way.

She shimmied out of her bra and let it fall between them, pressing against him the best she could, the heat of his body hardening her nipples in an instant. He released a shuddery breath, his hands moving from her back to her sides, skating over the farthest edges of her breasts. She leaned back again, hoping he'd take the hint.

He did.

Warm hands covered her, his palms creating gentle friction as he squeezed.

Oh, yes. Just like that.

His mouth soon followed, one hand curving around her right breast as his tongue lapped against the peak with slow wet strokes.

She wanted him down on the bed, but when she tried to urge him in that direction, he stayed right where he was, suckling her until she thought she would explode from that alone.

"Blake, please." The words came at the end of a long moan.

Her fingers went to his buckle, and this time he didn't try to stop her. She threaded the end backward until it released. Pushing it aside, she found the button on his khakis and fiddled with it, finally getting it through the hole. *Almost there.* He kissed his way to her other breast. Applied gentle suction. A wave of pleasure swept over her, and her hands went slack under the onslaught, all rational thought fleeing. It took several seconds to find her place and the tab of his zipper.

Zip!

The sound pulled Blake up short, and he looked into her eyes. "Last chance to back out."

Was he serious?

"That chance came and went a long time ago."

He chuckled, but it sounded strained. "Good, I'm glad you said that."

Easing her down onto the bed—something she'd tried to get him to do a few minutes ago with no success—he undid her slacks in record time, skimming them and her panties over her legs and letting them drop to the floor.

She flung out a hand, searching for the clear plastic bag.

"I have it," he murmured, standing and divesting himself of the rest of his clothing. When he came back down, he was already covered. A flicker of disappointment went over her when her hand closed around him. She'd wanted to feel every silky hard inch of him with no barriers between them. At least with her hand, if nothing else.

Next time. He'd promised her until this afternoon.

His palm brushed over her stomach in light gentle strokes, moving closer inch by inch. Her hips pushed up, needing something he seemed determined to withhold. She tightened her hand around him and the hissing sound of his indrawn breath made her smile. Two could play at this game.

Then he touched her, and all bets were off. His fingers drew something wild up from the pit of her stomach, but before she had time to put a name to it, he'd parted her legs and thrust into her.

Hard. Before she'd had time to think, to prepare…to hold off.

Her breath exploded from her lungs as a torrent of sensation ripped through her, her fingers digging into his back as she clenched around him again and again. He buried his face in her neck and groaned out her name, the sound agonized as he rode with her up the crest…followed her over the edge.

The weight of his body was the only thing anchoring her to the bed, to the earth—and she clung to him for all she was worth, waiting for her frantic heartbeats to slow. Blake's lips touched her neck in light, brushing kisses that worked magic on her soul.

"Sorry," he murmured, his breath warm against her skin.

She turned her head so her chin rested on his cheek. "For what?"

"I meant that to last a lot longer."

"Yeah. Me, too." She couldn't hold back the laugh, so glad he hadn't apologized for making love to her. Or for anything else. A quick arrival she could handle. Regret she couldn't.

She slid her hands down his back, his skin moist even though the room was cool.

Rolling to the side, he took her with him, dragging the bedspread over both of them.

A huge yawn rolled through her despite her best efforts to hold it at bay, drawing a chuckle from him. Between flying to Anchorage and back and caring for a critical patient, she was suddenly exhausted.

He smoothed her hair back, and something about the gesture touched her, just as it had the other times he'd done it. "Sleep," he said.

If she did, this day would end far too soon. But her eyelids were heavy. Already drifting shut. "Wake me later?" she whispered on a sigh.

"You can count on it."

"Don't tell anyone at the clinic about this, okay?"

He smiled. How many things had she asked him to keep to himself so far? Three? Four? The list was growing fast. And heaven help him, if he didn't want it to keep on growing.

Blake gave her a quick kiss as he cleared away the dishes from a very late lunch. "It'll be our secret."

"That's right, Mister Fighter Pilot, you said you were good at those." Propping her elbows on the counter, the motion of her hips twisted the barstool back and forth, the tails of his dress shirt parting to reveal a tantalizing length of leg. He'd handed her the garment after she'd got up, so she'd have something to wear while her other clothes went through the washer and dryer.

Damn.

Three times, and he still wanted her. How could that be? A twinge of apprehension came over him. Some things should definitely be kept to himself.

"Secrets and I are like this." He crossed his fingers, using the symbol to reassure himself as well as her.

Being with a woman couldn't be this simple. Not for him. He was the master of jumping into things with both eyes shut and then coming to rue them in the cold light of day.

Like Molly?

His teeth ground together. He hoped not. This was one night he didn't want to look back on with regret.

She hopped off her barstool. "I'll help clean up."

"When do you want to get back?"

"Soon." She wrinkled her nose. "I probably should head over to the house and put on a different set of clothes."

"I'll take you." Glancing at his watch, he found himself

glad to put a little space between them. He couldn't think with her swiveling back and forth on that stool, because it brought up thoughts of her swiveling back and forth on him. Something they didn't have time for. "Do you want to shower here, or wait until you get home?"

"Here." She sent him a smile. "Want to join me?"

He gave a rough laugh that he hoped sounded pained. "I never thought I'd say this, but I think you've worn me out."

It was a lie, and he knew it. His body was ready to take her again and a shower sounded…

Dangerous. Far too intimate. To be standing under the hot pounding spray with nothing between them but soapy lather, and slick needy bodies…

Hell, what was wrong with him?

It was too soon. He'd jumped the gun. Again. He should have waited until he knew for sure she was going to stay, because if she suddenly balked—suddenly decided she couldn't handle flying any more—he was screwed. Or if she decided she wanted to go back to Anchorage, it would be even worse.

Unaware of his thoughts, she pulled the shirt a little lower over her thighs. "Your loss." Walking toward the bathroom, the saucy twitch of her hips was full of invitation. "If you change your mind, you know where I'll be."

As soon as she was out of sight—the door to the bathroom clicking shut—he threw the dishrag on the counter and dragged a hand through his hair. His body was an inferno of need, his chest aching with something he dared not define.

She was brave, resourceful, willing to face her fears—so far.

Was she out of that shirt yet?

The sound of the shower turning on confirmed she was. He grew harder.

Time to recite all the reasons he shouldn't go in there.

He stood in the center of his kitchen, not a single thought coming to mind. He tried. Really he did.

You shouldn't go in there because...

Ah, hell. He left the dishes on the bar and headed for the bathroom. If he was going to screw up his life, he might as well finish the job.

CHAPTER SIXTEEN

"HEY, is this hard?" Molly picked up a video game case that was lying on a bookshelf as she waited for him to get dressed. Her legs were having a dickens of a time holding her up, and she'd been forced to walk around, trying to convince her muscles to do their job.

He peered around the corner of his closet door and gave her a smile. "Not yet. But it could be."

She lobbed a pillow at him. "I meant this."

Crossing over to her, he glanced at the cover. "A flight simulator?"

"You got me thinking." She turned the cover over and read the description. "I said I couldn't fly even if you were passed out at the wheel. I was joking at the time, but what if it really happened? Or what if you were incapacitated?"

His brows lifted. "You mean like now?"

"I'm serious." A laugh came out and belied the words.

He took the case from her hands and stared at the cover. "We can try it out if you want, but I thought you weren't interested in flying. That you were going to tolerate it for the sake of your job."

Yes, she'd meant those words at the time, but a subtle shift had taken place. Not only had her father loved flying but it was Blake's life. And because of that...

No, don't go there. Not yet.

But even as the thought whispered through her mind, she was already searching for an excuse to see him again. To not walk away and forget this morning ever happened.

But why? They'd still be working together, so they'd have to see each other.

But it wouldn't be the same. She'd lose something special once she left this house. They might have known each other for a few short weeks, but if Blake considered their time together a one-night stand...

Surely not. She'd sensed something desperate in his love-making that last time in the shower, as if he was fighting something inside himself. Whatever it was, it hadn't stopped him from bracing his hands against the tile and bringing their time together to a shattering conclusion.

One that had left her limp and shaking.

He'd had to wrap his arms around her to keep from sliding to the floor in a heap. In the harsh light of day, the memory sent a shiver of fear through her. She'd never experienced goodbye sex before, but it was probably pretty similar to what they'd done.

Hello and goodbye all in the space of twelve hours. Maybe he was the smart one.

"When are you off next?" he asked.

"Not until Saturday." Almost a week away.

"I could come over and install the game on your computer, if you'd like. Show you how to work it. Then you could try it out at your leisure."

She paused. "I could make us lunch."

"Will it involve horseradish?"

Molly laughed again, remembering his reaction to Jed's sandwich. "You'll have to wait and see. Think of it as expanding your horizons." She tapped the game he held in his hand. "Something we should both consider doing."

* * *

The week crawled by, and Blake didn't appear at the clinic once. Neither did he call. By Friday morning her mood had slid downhill, landing at the bottom with a splat.

She met Sammi outside the exam room with a scowl. "Nail guns should not be sold without a permit."

The CHA held out the set of pliers Molly had asked her to hunt down. "Hey, *I* have a nail gun at home."

"Yeah, but you didn't use it to fasten your hand to a crate on one of the fishing boats." She rolled her eyes. "How is it that a man who can open a beer bottle with his teeth can't stand the thought of pulling a nail out of his own hand?"

Sammi winced. "Sounds like someone I know could use some chocolate. Mark hasn't called?"

"What?"

"You said you went out with him a couple of weeks ago." The other woman studied the bright yellow polish on her nails.

It took Molly a minute to even remember the date. "We did, but I think we're destined to be friends. Nothing more." All she could hope was that Sammi hadn't heard about her spending a large chunk of time at Blake's house.

No one knew. And he'd sworn he'd never tell.

Although why it was okay for Sammi to pair her up with Mark and not Blake she had no idea. Maybe because she was still smarting from needing to be with him more than he evidently wanted to be with her.

Hurt swept through her.

Sammi touched her shoulder, bringing her back to the present. "You okay?"

"Fine." She sighed. "The clinic's just been busy this week."

"I heard the head injury patient is going to recover. The blown pupil was from a previous eye injury. I thought it was from being hit by the crab pot."

"Me, too." She squeezed the other woman's arm. "Hey, listen. I'm sorry for being such a grouch."

"Don't worry about it. It happens." Sammi shrugged. "What are you doing this weekend?"

She wasn't sure. Blake had said he'd come over on Saturday and install the flight simulator on her computer, but she had no idea if that was still on or not. "Samita and I are going to lounge around the house and be lazy."

"If you get bored, call and we can do something."

"Thanks, Sammi, I will." Being with her new friend would definitely be better than moping around all day. "I need to get back to my patient."

Fifteen minutes of wrestling and her patient's hand was free of the board and the nail. She examined the wound again. The metal had shot into the space between the second and third metacarpals. No actual bone involvement, just skin. A stitch or two, a tetanus shot, and some antibiotics, and he'd be as good as new.

"I'd like you to give this hand a break for a few days," she said as she sutured both the entry and exit wounds.

"My captain's already threatened to kick my butt if I touch that gun again. He lost almost a whole day bringing me back in to have it looked at." He checked out the repair and closed his hand into an experimental fist. "Doesn't hurt at all."

Molly dropped the needle and tweezers back onto the tray to be sterilized and stood, patting his shoulder. "Wait until the lidocaine wears off. You're going to want to take some ibuprofen before that happens—six hundred milligrams worth—in about an hour." She smiled. "But at least you won't be carrying a board around with you any more."

He glanced at the instrument tray. "Uh…Doc. You don't suppose I could have that nail you plucked from me, do you? I want to show it to my boys."

Her brows went up. "On one condition."

"Yeah, what's that?"

"That you promise to teach them about tool safety and practice it yourself from here on out."

The burly fisherman gave her a sheepish grin. "It's a deal."

Rinsing off the offending nail and then dropping it into his hand, they both stood. Her patient slid the sharp object into the front pocket of his worn jeans, causing her to cringe. Hopefully he would remember it was there before getting into his car to drive away. She really, *really* didn't want to have to pull it out of him again—especially not from that region. "Take care, okay?"

"Will do."

Pushing through the room's heavy door, Molly watched him walk toward the reception area.

A few strands of hair fell over her forehead, and she shoved them back, the locks feeling as lank and lifeless as she did. She moved into the hallway and turned right, heading in the same direction her patient had.

"You busy?"

The familiar voice caused her heart to skip a beat. She stopped in her tracks, then spun around, finding Blake standing behind her, arms folded across his chest. "You scared me. Where did you come from?"

"Sammi said you had a patient, so I thought I'd wait for you in the hall. Anything serious?"

"Nothing a two by four to the head wouldn't cure."

On second thought, maybe she could use one of those herself, judging from the way her heart was still ricocheting around in her chest at the sight of him.

"Ouch. Bad day?"

"About normal for a Friday." She could be distant, too. Really she could.

He nodded, studying her face for a moment. "Are we still on for tomorrow?"

It took her a minute to realize he was talking about coming over to her house for lunch. Somehow it really miffed her that he hadn't offered any explanation for his absence, or even tried to see her. "Sure. If you're still up for it."

"I am." He paused as if trying to come up with the right words. "Listen, sorry I haven't been around. I don't want you to think…"

Everything inside her clenched. Was he about to give her the we've-had-some-fun-but-let's-just-be-friends speech?

Holding up a hand, she tried to head him off. "Don't worry about it."

A small frown appeared between his brows, and he lowered his voice. "I started to come by the clinic a couple of times, but I remembered what you said about keeping our time together a secret. I didn't think you'd want me hanging around."

I didn't think you'd want me hanging around. Those words made her tummy do a back flip. So that was why he'd stayed away.

She did want him to hang around. Very much.

She gave him a smile. "I thought you were going to say… Never mind."

"Then I had to go to Fairbanks on Wednesday and Thursday."

"A patient?" Surely she would have heard or been asked to go along.

"No. I had some property that's been up for sale for a while. The Realtor finally found a buyer, and I had to meet my ex-wife to sign the papers."

Relief turned to dismay. He'd met his ex-wife and stayed for two days? How long did it take to sign a piece of paper?

You're being unreasonable, Molly. He just said he was thinking about coming by the clinic.

"That's okay. Did the sale go through?"

He glanced down the hallway, then tugged a lock of her hair, letting it fall back in place. "It did. I'm glad that's over."

If he was glad, she was glad. Except he'd made no move to kiss her.

Why would he? She'd asked him to keep things quiet. Besides, no sense in either of them getting too serious. They were colleagues. That was one strike. A second strike was that the hospital might not even renew her contract at the clinic after the year was up. Which meant she'd end up…not in Anchorage, where she might still see Blake from time to time, but in some other city. Probably in the lower forty-eight.

Where she'd never see him again.

Her heart tumbled even as she smiled and said she'd see him tomorrow.

Two strikes. One more and Molly would be forced to call it a day.

She needed to pray that she could pull herself back together if that happened.

CHAPTER SEVENTEEN

BLAKE used his elbow to ring the bell, his hands full of flight-simulator equipment.

The door opened a few seconds later, and Molly, dressed in snug jeans and a green silky top with some kind of fluttery sleeves, smiled in welcome, Samita by her side. Her feet were bare, soft pink polish on her toenails.

No music came from inside today, which was a good thing. Although those dainty toes…

He swallowed. Maybe this wasn't such a good idea after all.

"Come in."

Too late to run now. He'd gone out last night for some liquid courage, hoping to get up the nerve to call her and say he'd had second thoughts. He'd run into Mark at the bar and immediately tensed, but his buddy had surprised him by clapping him on the back and wishing him luck.

"With what?" he'd asked.

Mark had responded with raised eyebrows, slugging back his first shot of whiskey and then asking for another.

His friend knew.

The serial dater of Dutch Harbor was actually stepping aside instead of pursuing a woman who'd caught his interest. The agreement passed between the two old friends without a word being said. Blake used to think Mark and Sammi had something special going on, but after Mark had come home from the military something changed between them. The two barely spoke any more.

He came back to the present with a bump, realizing Molly was still waiting for him to enter the house. She took some of the items from his hands as he moved past her. "The computer's in the living room."

The scent of some kind of grilled meat permeated the air, making his mouth water. "Whatever you're making smells delicious."

"Pork chops. They should be ready in a few minutes."

Leading him to an oak, slant-front desk with delicate curved legs, she folded down the front panel, revealing a laptop computer inside. "I hope this is okay."

"It's fine."

She paused for a second, and an awkward silence ensued. "Do you think you could set it up while I finish lunch?"

"Not a problem."

He pulled the computer forward onto the desktop, and waited for it to boot up. Glancing around the room, he noted everything was neatly put away—no more boxes lining the walls. She didn't have a lot of furniture, but what she did have looked comfortable.

A beige leather sofa, paired with a rustic plank coffee table, sat under the picture window, its sleek lines adding a modern touch to the traditional space. On top of the coffee table a trio of chunky candles had been arranged on a silver tray, a manila folder resting beside them. A small flatscreened television perched on a narrow table against an adjacent wall.

He smiled. The TV looked like a miniature version of his own. Men and women seemed to have different priorities in life. He couldn't imagine watching the Super Bowl on a screen that size. The players would look like ants.

He turned back to the computer, finding it ready to use.

He first installed the program and then set up the yoke and pedals just as Molly walked into the dining area, carrying a platter. "Are you ready to eat?"

"Yep. Can I help?"

"The salad is on the counter in the kitchen. Would you mind bringing it in?"

Blake found a crystal bowl housing an assortment of greens and tomatoes. His stomach growled at the sight. He hadn't realized how hungry he was.

"It's just down-home cooking, hope that's all right," Molly said as he joined her.

"I can't think of anything better."

A line of plump pork chops—a sauce of some kind drizzled down the center of the tray—fired up his salivary glands. Along the outside of the chops lay new potatoes, a sliver of skin peeled away from each one.

It had been ages since he'd had a meal like this one. He normally subsisted on sandwiches or prepackaged meals. Seeing Molly standing there, her hands twisting together in uncertainty, made his chest ache with a strange sense of longing.

"Do you want wine? Or would you rather have iced tea?"

Neither. He wanted her.

But no way was he going to say that. He'd already decided he needed to hang back for a while and see how things went. His jump-in-with-both-feet tendencies were officially on vacation. "Wine would be great."

She handed him a glass, and they sat at the table. The meal was delicious, but his eyes were on Molly as she talked about her week at the clinic and asked about his work. She leaned forward, focusing intently on him as if she really cared what his boring day-to-day routine involved.

Enough about him.

"So how are you finding the islands so far?"

She sat back, sipping her wine. "They're different than I

expected." She must have seen his frown, because she quickly added, "In a good way. I love Sammi and working at the clinic. The pace is just slower than what I'm used to."

"Unless we have an emergency." He remembered how lost she'd seemed at the hospital after they'd delivered their head-injury patient into the hands of other doctors. "Then it can be crazy for a while."

"Definitely." She paused, before setting her glass down. "Listen, about the way I ran out of the hospital the other day, I know I must have seemed totally off my rocker, but Gary, my ex, is persistent. We stopped seeing each other six months ago, but between him and my mother...well, let's just say I was happy when this job opened up."

"You don't have to explain." But it did answer a question that had lingered in his mind. She'd said she wanted to make peace with what her father had done, but he hadn't been able figure out why she'd waited until four years after his death to do that.

She shrugged. "Just thought you should know, in case it happens again. I'm sure we'll have more patients to trans-port."

"Is he harassing you?"

"No, he's not calling me any more, if that's what you mean. He just makes it a point to run into me at work." Her laugh was pained. "And my mom likes him—always has. Besides, he's firmly planted in Anchorage. It would take a natural di-saster to uproot him."

"So *you* left instead."

"That pretty much sums it up." She cleared her throat. "So, moving on to another subject. What did you think of the sauce?"

Blake put his napkin on the table. "I think my empty plate speaks for itself."

"It had horseradish in it."

"You're kidding." The sauce had been mild and creamy with the barest hint of tang. Nothing like the molten lava he remembered his mom serving with roast beef.

"Nope." She smiled and sipped at her wine. "Like I said, maybe you should expand your horizons."

"Maybe I should." His eyes met hers and held, as they'd done several times during the meal.

She cleared her throat. "Well, if you're ready, we can take our drinks into the living room and you can show me how to work the game. I know you said you weren't interested in helping me through a twelve-step program, so I won't make you sit there and watch me."

"It's okay. We can just look at it as fun, with a little therapy thrown in for free."

They carried their wine into the living room. Samita, who'd been lounging on the coffee table, her front feet on the manila folder, glanced up at them and yawned.

"What if I crash?" she asked.

"We'll take some easy routes with nice long runways and work our way up to the challenging stuff."

Her brows went up, and she took another sip of wine. "We can accomplish that all in one day?"

"No, but we could work on it a little at a time."

Now that he'd said it, he realized what a royally stupid idea it was. He took a hefty swig of his wine. Why subject himself to the torture of sitting shoulder to shoulder with her, helping her handle the flight stick, when it was already putting all kinds of thoughts in his mind?

"Sounds like twelve steps to me," she muttered.

"Maybe it'll be a shorter version. Two or three steps." He set his glass down and started the program.

Molly dragged a chair from the dining room and sat next to him. Her scent surrounded him, bringing back memories of tangled limbs and the desperate kisses they'd shared a week ago.

Hell.

He should have taken her to a public place like a video arcade, but since he already had the game this had seemed like a good idea.

Yeah. A great one.

Kind of like the decision he'd made to put his arm around her and comfort her when she'd found the picture of her father on his wall.

Comfort her. What a crock.

A quick fling had seemed easy and painless when his lips had been welded to hers. But it hadn't been. He'd realized that the second they'd pulled away from each other.

"This was really nice of you, Blake."

"You might not think so after an hour or two."

He positioned the chair to have access to the rudder pedals he'd placed on the floor beneath their impromptu work area.

"Okay, you can sit here in front of the computer."

She licked her lips. "Could you do the takeoff, and I'll just fly it for a minute or two—under optimal conditions?"

"Sure." A sick feeling worked its way through his chest. One screw-up on his part, and he could make everything worse—could make her more afraid than ever. What had started out as a game suddenly seemed deadly serious.

He selected the absolute easiest program on the list. Molly leaned closer, the warmth and the scent of her shampoo flowed through him, lingering in places it didn't belong. It took everything he had not to lean closer and draw it deep into his lungs. "You can help me throttle up, how's that?"

As long as he didn't allow *himself* to get any more throttled up than he already was.

The screen flickered and showed a Cessna sitting on a

long stretch of runway. "Do you want the view from inside the cockpit or outside?"

"You choose."

"Inside. It'll seem more realistic."

Her nose crinkled. "Great."

He couldn't hold back a smile. "It won't be as bad as you think."

"I'll hold you to that."

Switching the view, he tapped the throttle controls. "This is where much of your engine power comes from." He showed her how to increase and decrease the prop speed until she was able to hear the high-pitched whine that signaled they had enough power. "Ready?"

"I hope so."

"We're going to taxi into position." He used the foot pedals to turn the plane on the screen. Once he was lined up with the centerline of the runway, he took her hand and placed it on the throttle along with his, the coolness of her fingers in direct contrast to his overheated senses.

"We're going to take off. Push the throttle in, slowly. That's it." The speed increased, the plane moving forward. "Once we reach around sixty miles per hour, I'll pull back on the yoke to get the nose into the air."

The virtual plane moved faster and faster. Long runways like this one bored him under normal circumstances, but something in him felt energized today. Molly would experience a little of the thrill that he did on each takeoff. He couldn't look into her face to see if she was enjoying the experience or terrified as the wheels left the ground. "Now I'll straighten out a little bit, climbing slowly." He readjusted the throttle then let go of her hand to tap the altimeter on the screen. "When this reads six thousand five hundred feet, we'll start leveling off by pushing the yoke forward until the plane is flying straight. We can go as high as twelve thousand feet, but we won't today."

"My heart is in my throat right now, and I'm not even doing the flying. Is that normal?"

"There is no normal. Every flight is different."

It was true of flying. Maybe it was true of relationships as well.

Once they were at cruising altitude, he switched places with her. "All you'll need to do is keep it in the air. We'll do some easy turns. You don't have to worry about other planes. It's just you and me. With the sky all to ourselves."

Her head swiveled to glance at him for a second, her pupils widening before she turned back to the screen.

Okay, so the *sky to ourselves* narrative could have been stated a little differently. His attraction was already outside the boundaries he'd established for himself, and growing fast. And seeing her behind the controls of the plane only made it worse—played a mind game on him that could easily send everything spinning out of control.

He cleared his throat. "Let's start banking to the right."

"What?"

"We're going to make a turn. You'll steer like you would a car, but do it gradually. Nothing fast. You want the wing on the right side to dip slightly, then we'll raise it back up when we're ready to fly straight again."

Her teeth dug into her lip as she concentrated. "At least there are no road bumps when fake flying."

He grinned. "We can vary the weather conditions, if you'd like."

"No!" She glanced back at him, then saw he was joking. "Don't even say that. I don't want to crash my first time out."

Neither did he. Only his crashing had nothing to do with flying and everything to do with the woman seated next to him. "You're doing great. Now straighten back out."

She turned too fast and the right wing bumped up, then went about twenty degrees above the horizon. A tiny yelp came from her throat as she realized what she'd done. He laid a hand on one of hers and helped her bring the plane back under control.

A half hour later, when she seemed a little more relaxed, he decided to end on a good note. "First step accomplished. You flew a plane. Are you ready to head back to the airport so we can land this thing?"

"Only if you're the one in control."

His body leapt for a second, and he had to remind himself they were talking about landing. Nothing else.

He directed her to do another wide swinging turn—which she aced this time. He upped the cruising speed so the return flight would take less time. "See? You're getting it."

Her mouth quirked to the left. "Yeah. I'm a regular stunt pilot."

He laughed. "Not quite. But could you have pictured yourself doing this a couple of weeks ago?"

"No." She shrugged. "But then again, I couldn't imagine myself ever wanting to take this job a month ago. And it took a dare for me to actually get on the plane."

"A dare?"

She nodded. "When we got to the airport that first morning I chickened out, said I couldn't go through with it. My friend Doug had to double-dare me to get on the plane." She must have noticed his confusion because she continued, "We've been friends a long time. He knows how to push my buttons."

Friendships could turn into something else. Once the thought went through his head, he grimaced. What was with him?

"What?" Molly stared at him.

"Nothing."

"You rolled your eyes." Her lips tightened. "Sorry if that seems a little childish to you, but it did get me on the plane."

If he told her what he was really disgusted at, she'd be out of there faster than you could say *Assume crash positions*— something he wasn't quite ready to do.

He slid his hand across the one gripping the wheel, covering it and holding the plane in position. "Molly, look at me."

When she did, he mustered up all the sincerity he could and let it shine through his gaze. "I promise, I wasn't making fun of you. I think you've done an awesome job today. You proved you could do something you never dreamed possible."

She looked back at him for a few seconds, then the fingers beneath his parted, allowing his fingers to drop between hers. The plane on the screen jiggled for a second at the change in pressure. Unaware of what had happened, she squeezed his hand. "Thank you."

His breath stalled for a second. Did she realize they were almost holding hands? He didn't want to move. Let their little plane run out of gas and plow into the ground for all he cared.

None of this was real. Nothing but the touch of her skin against his. The pressing of flesh to flesh.

He forced himself to ease his fingers from hers. "We should be almost to the airport."

"Okay, tell me what to do." Her eyes went back to the screen.

He saw the runway in the distance. "You're going to overshoot the airport on this pass, so we'll have time to switch places." He glanced at her. "Unless you want to attempt the landing yourself?"

"No. Just...no."

Scooting the foot pedals back under the table, he got ready for the change of positions. He put his hand back on the yoke, well away from where her fingers were this time. "Okay,

I've got the wheel. Go ahead and move to your left. I'll take it from here."

She got up, and he changed seats with her, rearranging things and banking into the turn. As he pulled back around, he lined the plane up with the runway, explaining what he was doing, just like he'd done during their takeoff. He made a smooth descent, landing the plane with a minimal flickering of the screen.

"There, all safe and sound." He taxied off the runway, then powered down the plane. Swiveling in his chair, he found her staring at him.

A soft flush had stolen across her cheeks, and her lips were stained a deep pink, either from gnawing on them during the flight or from some other reason. He didn't much care which at the moment. All he knew was that the woman was gorgeous.

She took his breath away, like no other woman ever had.

"You okay?" he asked, half afraid of the answer.

"I think so…" She ran a hand through her short locks, the motion pulling the green shirt taut against her breasts.

His mouth went dry as she met his gaze and slowly lowered her hand. "Do you know what this means?"

Yes, and he could kick himself for bringing her here, where all he wanted to do was take her to bed and kiss her senseless. He needed to say something, but what?

"No, what does it mean?"

Her eyes glittered, and he prayed those weren't tears of fear. Or anger.

"Blake…I can fly."

CHAPTER EIGHTEEN

HE CUPPED her face with gentle hands. "You can fly."

The memory of those hands running over her body as they'd made love last week rose up in her chest…along with all the other emotions he'd dragged from deep inside her.

This was a man who was fearless, unafraid to pitch in where he was needed, even on Jed's gruesome injury. And of all the daredevil professions he could have chosen—sky-diver, deep-sea fisherman, ski instructor—he'd chosen one that not only thrilled him but saved lives. That seemed to go along with being a rescue pilot, his EMS work, and even his combat training. All designed to serve and protect others.

A lump clogged her throat. This man was…

Oh, Lord, was it possible to fall in love this fast?

Her stomach turned over in a way that had nothing to do with the meal she'd just eaten.

It wasn't love. It couldn't be.

It had to be their shared experiences: the danger of Jed's rescue; the trip to Akutan; his patience in showing her how to use the flight program.

The knot in her throat tightened. She needed to give herself a little space to think. Make that a lot of space.

Hard to do with him looking at her like he wanted to devour her.

As if he sensed the tangle of emotions he'd generated inside her, he murmured, "I know we kind of did this backward, and I wouldn't blame you if you decided you wanted no part of any of this. But…"

She bit her lip. "But?"

Letting go of her, he rubbed the back of his hand along his jaw. "If I asked you out, on a date, would you say yes?"

Of all the things he could have said, this was the last thing she'd expected. "*If* you asked me out? Are you?"

"Only if you're planning to say yes."

Her heart lightened, and a shaft of joy went through her. "What happened to that daredevil blood you claimed to have? The stuff that tells you to take a chance?"

"It sometimes deserts me at the worst possible time."

She smiled. "Okay, so ask me and see what happens."

"I know things have been a little awkward ever since… well…last week. But would you go out with me tomorrow? If you're not working, that is."

"I'm not."

"In that case, I'd like to take you to dinner. I know a good place."

"That's because there's *only* one place."

His face changed, going very serious. "Is that a problem?"

"No. I happen to love that particular restaurant."

"I'm glad." He took a deep breath and then got to his feet. "I think I'd better go. If I don't I'm going to ruin all my good intentions."

"What about your flight program?"

He stroked his fingers down her cheek sending a shiver over her. "Don't worry, Molly. I know where you live."

She stared in the mirror over her dresser, trying to decide if she looked lightly made up or like some sort of freakish clown. She fluffed her hair one last time, then sighed. There was nothing else she could do but wait for Blake and hope for the best.

Hope for the best.

Did she dare? She'd never thought she'd ever date another colleague. Or a pilot. And Blake was both.

Anticipation built slowly within her chest. He'd asked her out. Something that had taken her by surprise.

You know you wanted him to, Molly. Stop trying to fool yourself.

Now, if she could just go slowly, like he seemed to want. Because all *she* wanted to do was rip the man's clothes off and take him right there on her bed.

But she wouldn't. For a daredevil, he sure had a lot of common sense when it came to the important stuff. She needed to trust him.

Samita leapt on top of the dresser, head butting her chin when Molly bent down to her level.

"Silly girl." She hugged the animal close. "You are cute, though."

Setting the cat on the floor, she headed into the living room and sat on the couch, staring at the manila folder that was still on the coffee table. Within it lay her future. Something she didn't want to think about right now.

It was getting dark outside, so she went over to pull down the shades, seeing Blake's car pull into the driveway as she did. Her heart stumbled for a step or two, before taking off at a run. She gave a little wave and slid the shade the rest of the way down, before moving to open the door.

When he came up the walkway, damp hair slicked back from his face and a bouquet of flowers clutched in his right hand, he took her breath away. Why did he have to be so gorgeous? Even his civilized khakis and polo did nothing to detract from the image of raw masculinity. This was a man who could ride out the apocalypse and come through unscathed on the other side.

"Thank you." She somehow managed to get the words out as she took the flowers—a mixture of Gerber daisies and tiny pink roses. They were already arranged in a vase, which was a good thing, since she didn't remember packing one. Hers was probably still at her mother's house, boxed up with the remainder of her things. "Come in while I get my jacket and purse."

Samita trotted into the room and rubbed against his leg, drawing a laugh from Molly. "You do have a way with women."

He bent down to pet the animal, and she finally noticed he hadn't said a word. If anything, his solemnity was a bit unnerving. Maybe he was as jittery as she was.

And she was a mess.

"Are you all right?" she asked, setting the flowers on the coffee table.

"Fine." He stood, his eyes finally meeting hers, sliding over her beige cashmere sweater and chocolate-colored slacks. "You look lovely."

The way he said it put her on alert. "Thank you. You don't look too shabby yourself."

He cupped her face, thumbs sliding along her cheekbones as he'd done when she'd successfully conquered the flight simulator. The intensity in his touch made something flip in her chest. Before she could react, he leaned in, pressing his cheek to hers and inhaling deeply.

Her hands automatically cupped his nape and held him to her.

"You're a special woman." His breath warmed her ear sending a shiver through her. "You deserve so much out of life. So much more than I…"

The half-finished phrase and his obvious struggle to get

the words out made her knees quake. Was he getting ready to drop the ax on whatever had begun between them?

Oh, God.

"If you're having second thoughts, I understand."

He drew a shuddery breath, then his lips trailed along her jaw. "No second thoughts."

Relief swamped her, changing quickly to need. Drugged by his touch, she shifted to intercept his mouth as it continued on its path. It worked. His lips slid over hers, and electricity shot through her, burning from her lips to her very core. She wanted him. Needed to hold him to her so he wouldn't drift away. It wasn't rational, but the sudden press of fear didn't allow for coherent thought.

Her fingers burrowed deeper into his hair, while she pressed her body to his. The heat coming off him was incredible and every hard inch of him felt ready for business.

Yes, that was more like it.

He pulled back slightly. "Dinner, remember?"

Her lips ached where he'd kissed her, and her heart beat a wild rhythm inside her chest. "How hungry are you?"

"Very." The passion in his eyes testified to a very different kind of hunger.

The strong pulse of a vein in his neck drew her, and she lifted on tiptoe to slide her tongue along it, relishing the clean taste of his skin, the steady beat matching that of his heart. Reaching the top of his jaw, she nibbled it. "Let's eat in."

His fingers tangled in her hair, drawing her mouth away from him. "Hell, woman, I can't think while you're doing that."

"Mmm. That's the whole idea."

Was she crazy? Maybe. But kissing him was addictive. And like any addict, she craved more.

He held her there, his lips inches away. "If we stay here any longer, you're going to miss a meal. Maybe several."

The slightly threatening edge to his voice made her legs go wobbly and left her eager to see exactly where that warning might lead.

"I'm willing to risk it."

"Molly, hell, I… You're so beautiful." His throat worked as he swallowed. "I want you like I've never wanted any other woman."

Not even his ex-wife. The words hung between them for several seconds before her eyes misted. She needed to affirm the sentiment. "Me, too."

The next several seconds were a blur, and Molly wasn't sure who moved first, but suddenly they were in each other's arms, mouth on mouth, hands searching, exploring. Heartbeats collided as Molly struggled to stay afloat in the onslaught.

"Bed," she managed between breaths.

"Shh."

In the end she needn't have worried. Blake stripped her of her clothes piece by piece, kissing each exposed area as it appeared. Then, holding her hands, he drew her into the bedroom, pushing the door shut to hold the cat at bay. He released her just long enough to shrug out of his own clothes before sitting on the edge of the bed. His rigid flesh was right there. Bare. She wanted to feel it beneath her hand, in her.

Unable to resist, she stroked him, reveling in the strength that lay beneath that velvety soft layer of skin, in the low sound he made in his throat as she slowly tightened her grip. But when she went to kneel before him, he wrapped his hands around her upper arms, stopping her.

"Not this time." His voice came out as a low growl. "I want you up here. With me."

At his urging, she straddled him, taking the package he held in his hand and sheathing him, making sure she drew out the process until he groaned out a protest between clenched teeth.

Still holding him, she lowered onto him until all she felt was him filling her, his hands on her breasts, kneading, coaxing, using them to guide the speed and depth at which she took him in. She was on top, and yet Blake controlled her every move. Her every sensation.

And when she couldn't stand it any longer, she threw her head back and let go, releasing on a long keening note as his hands urged her to take him deeper, harder until, with a muttered oath, he thrust into her one last time, tumbling after her into oblivion.

Molly awoke to find herself sprawled across Blake's chest—still on her bed, his hand at her back holding her to him. Her arm dangled off the side, and when she moved, she was startled to find they hadn't uncoupled.

She gulped. And he was still hard. How long had she been asleep? Turning her head, she found him very much awake, his crooked smile tugging at her heart.

"I wouldn't wiggle around, if I were you."

Her hips gave an experimental pump, the sensation bringing a gasp from her lips. And a low curse from his.

"You mean like this?" she whispered.

He gripped her hips, holding her still while his teeth dug into her shoulder, his tongue lapping over the spot. This time her gasp morphed into a moan.

"That's what you get."

"Do it again."

Blake repeated the action a little to the right, his bite a little rougher this time before suckling the spot. Molly's senses blanked out for a second before roaring back to life.

Maybe there was something to those vampire books after all.

Would a doctor with a dozen hickeys really inspire confidence?

Oh, hell, she thought as he moved to the top of her left breast. *Did she really care?*

Something to the right of Blake's head churned to life, a familiar tune causing them both to freeze. He turned to look as her cellphone burst into song.

"Really?" Blake's brows went up.

"I have to get this, but..." she wiggled her hips again "...hold that thought."

She answered the phone, half laughing as his hands splayed across her bottom, cupping it as he grew even firmer inside her. "H-hello?"

"Dr. McKinna? This is Greta Benson, Darrin's wife."

Her mind drew a blank. Of course, it could be due to the warm tongue lapping along the joint of her shoulder.

The woman's voice came back through. "My husband came in with a spider bite a couple of weeks ago?"

"Oh, oh, yes." She held up a finger to Blake, asking him to give her a minute. She pulled away, gritting her teeth at the sense of emptiness the move brought about. Her robe was thrown across a nearby chair, and she pulled it on. "How can I help you?"

"Well, he hasn't checked his sugar today, and I need you to fuss at him."

Molly rolled her eyes. Oh, the joys of living in a small community. "Okay, put him on." She noted Blake had gotten out of bed and was pulling on his clothes.

Damn.

They hadn't had dinner yet. Maybe he was hungry.

She shook off her irritation at the interruption and focused on her patient.

Blake went into the living room to give Molly some privacy. He wandered around aimlessly for a minute or two before sitting on the sofa and picking up the remote. He'd come over here with a determination he hadn't felt in a long time. He wanted to give this thing with Molly a shot.

She wasn't Sharon. The more he was around her the more he realized she was cut out of very different cloth. She loved the islands, was coming to grips with going up in a plane. They could make this into an actual partnership.

At least he hoped that might be an option. He wanted to do more than just take her on a quick spin around the block—wanted much more than just two nights in her arms.

And damn if that didn't scare him at least as much as flying scared Molly.

He glanced at the remote in his hand, but before he could click the power button, Samita came running from somewhere in the kitchen, leaping toward the coffee table while still several yards away. Instead of landing squarely on the wooden surface, however, her paws hit the manila folder that was lying there, sending them both skidding off the edge.

Blake grinned when the cat made an irritated yowl in the back of her throat and glared at him as if he'd been personally responsible for the mishap, before stalking away with all the dignity she could muster. Papers had slid out of the folder and were strewn halfway across the room. He knelt and began gathering them, the letterhead on the top sheet drawing his attention.

Cleveland Clinic.

His eyes scanned the sheet for a second before realizing it was a letter responding to a request for information.

Dear Dr. McKinna,

Thank you for your interest in Cleveland Clinic. As a facility which offers world-class care, our physicians have access to cutting-edge research and...

He frowned and looked at the next letter in the stack—Duke University Medical Center.

There must be twenty letters from hospitals in major cities all over the United States. The one he was staring at was dated just a week ago. Right around the time they'd slept together for the first time.

Dread rose in his throat.

She was leaving. And she'd never said a word.

A sound made him look up. Molly stood in the doorway, a white terrycloth robe cinched tightly around her waist, her face almost as pale as the garment.

He stood, still holding the letters in his hand. "What are these?"

CHAPTER NINETEEN

S<small>HE</small>'D meant to put the folder away before he arrived, but had forgotten. She looked at his face, but saw nothing there, just a tight jaw and empty eyes.

"My contract with the clinic is only for a year. You knew that."

"If they don't extend it, I assumed you'd return to Alaska Regional—"

"No. I won't go back there." Not with the relationship with her mother the way it was. Not with Gary being there. She'd wanted a clean break, and she'd gotten it—loved the feeling of being her own person at last. If this job fell through, she'd be forced to move somewhere else. Even though everything she'd come to love was here in Unalaska.

Everything she loved…

An ache settled in her chest.

Blake dropped the papers onto the coffee table, not seeming to notice that the top sheet slid back onto the floor.

He moved to stand in front of her, not touching her. "What if I asked you to stay?"

The breath she'd been releasing caught in her throat and guilt flooded her. She couldn't think of an answer that would make sense to herself, much less to him. "I'm a doctor, Blake. What would I do here if I didn't practice medicine?"

"Maybe the clinic could hire you outright."

"They barely have enough funds to cover their month-to-month expenses. I can't justify asking them to pay me on top of that. Sammi is living on a pittance as it is." She stared at him, trying to come up with a solution, but her mind didn't seem to be functioning. She touched his face instead. "We still have almost eleven months, Blake."

"And after that?"

She dropped her hand. "I don't know." She studied the growing anger in his eyes and said quietly, "What if I asked you to give up your job? Give up what you love doing?"

"You wouldn't be the first one." The bitterness in his voice came through.

"Exactly. I don't *want* to be that person. Do you?"

He dragged a hand through his hair and turned away, swearing. He stood there, hands propped on his hips for a long time, ignoring Samita when she rubbed against his leg. When he finally turned back round, the anger was gone. In its place was a sense of quiet resignation. "No. I don't."

The second he stroked the back of his fingers across her jawline, the touch as soft as silk, she knew how this was going to end.

No. Don't do this!

"Goodbye, Molly."

The front door clicked shut behind him as he let himself out. Molly pressed both hands against her mouth to hold back the scream that bubbled up in her throat, the words whispering through her skull instead. *Please don't go.*

Blake leaned against his plane for what seemed like ages. He'd gone to the bar and sat there with two shots of whiskey lined up in front of him. But if he drank, he couldn't fly. And that was what he needed to do right now, fly as far away from Dutch Harbor as he could.

What the hell had he been thinking?

He'd been a fool. Thought he could have the rosy image of love—sitting on a mountainside, watching the sunset day after day.

But he wasn't his parents. There was no happy ending in sight. No retirements in Florida, no growing old together.

He should have learned his lesson the first time around.

Damn if Mark wasn't a whole lot smarter than he was. His friend didn't get involved, didn't hang around long enough to get hurt.

On some level he knew that wasn't exactly true, but his buddy had figured out a system that seemed to work. That was what Blake needed to do as well. Work out a system all of his own. He gave a hard laugh. Until then, flying off into the sunset was the best he could do.

Reaching into the pocket of his jacket, he found the lollipop he'd put there days ago. Looked like he wouldn't need to frame this thing after all. He'd finally learned his lesson. Had finally stopped digging.

Blake walked over to the trashcan and dropped the piece of candy inside. Then he turned toward his plane, climbed inside the cockpit and started his preflight check.

"Molly, slow down. I can barely keep up with you."

Resetting the length of her strides, she wound back her speed until she was jogging beside Sammi again. "Sorry. Where are all those endorphins you promised I'd start feeling?"

In reality, Molly didn't feel anything. A numbness had settled over her when Blake had walked out of her house three weeks ago that nothing had been able to penetrate.

"They…take time to kick in." Sammi's voice sounded strained. Molly had a feeling it was from more than just the running they'd been doing.

"Really? How long?"

The other woman laughed. "I don't know. I haven't actually experienced them myself either."

Molly stopped in her tracks. "Why the hell are we running, then? I could have been sleeping instead." She'd been doing a whole lot of that lately. Sleeping. The one place the numbness didn't matter. Molly knew it wasn't healthy, knew she was wading dangerously close to the line between a normal dose of grief following the end of a relationship and something more serious.

"Because it's good for us? That's what we tell all our patients, anyway." Sammi put her hands on her knees, trying to catch her breath.

Molly hadn't seen Blake since he'd left. Hadn't even tried to. And Sammi, sensing something was seriously wrong, had taken up the slack, going to the EMS department herself whenever they needed something. Blake must have felt the same, because the one medevac she'd done in the interim had been with another pilot. Someone named Ronny. She'd told herself it was for the best, that the frisson of disappointment that had gone through her was normal.

Normal.

Yeah. If she said the word enough times, that had to make it true.

She walked alongside her friend to cool down, hands on her hips. It was still early, and a thick fog had descended during the night. She knew the ocean was to her left, but she couldn't see it. She just heard the crashing of the waves as they beat against the rocks. "Can I ask you something?"

"Mmm."

"What would you do if the clinic closed?"

There was a minute or two of silence, then Sammi stopped and looked at her, water droplets from the mist clinging to her dark hair. "I don't know. Why?"

"Blake asked me to stay. Even if my contract isn't renewed."

The other woman's eyes widened. "He did? What did you say?"

"I told him I couldn't."

"So that's why…"

Molly eyed her. "Why what?"

She shook her head. "Nothing."

"Do you think I did the right thing?"

"I'm sorry, Molly, but I'm the last person you want to take advice from." She pulled her braid over her shoulder, wrapping it around her hand a couple of times. "I will say this, though. The one time I didn't listen to my heart, I made the biggest mistake of my life."

Listen to her heart.

What was it telling her to do?

She had no idea. It was numb like the rest of her. Molly looked deeper, the beating in her chest growing stronger, rising within her. No, it wasn't numb. She'd just tuned out its cries. It was telling her to do something that filled her with fear…and a strange sense of hope.

"I have to go to the EMS station."

Sammi blinked. "Why?"

"I have to tell Blake I'll stay. Somehow. I'll find a way."

"Oh, honey." Her friend's teeth came down on her lip. "I thought you knew."

"Knew what?"

"Blake's not at the department."

The tiny spark of hope sputtered. "What do you mean? Where is he?"

"He flew to Anchorage three weeks ago. No one's heard from him since."

What?

It was unfathomable that he would go away—leave the island. He loved it here. Loved his job.

And now he'd left it all behind.

Because of her.

Oh, God.

Her jaw firmed. No. No more crying. She had to make this right. She *would* make this right.

Somehow.

"Can you watch Samita for a day or two?"

"Sure, but what—?"

Molly turned around and started jogging back the way they'd come. "I have to go to Anchorage."

She'd only made it a few yards when Sammi's voice came through the fog behind her. "Call Mark. He'll take you."

CHAPTER TWENTY

BLAKE pressed "end" on his cellphone and scratched a line through another name on his list. Four down, sixteen or so left to go.

He'd been to hell and back during the three weeks he'd been away from Unalaska, but he'd also done a lot of thinking. He'd been selfish—and foolish—to expect Molly to change her whole life to accommodate his wants and needs.

This morning he'd come to a decision. Yes, he'd given up things for a woman before, but he'd resented each and every instance. Whenever Sharon asked for something more, his root of bitterness dug in a little deeper. And although he'd appeared to give in to her, he'd always held back part of himself. Not consciously, maybe, but he'd done it just the same. It was possible Sharon had sensed that. Maybe that was why she'd never been satisfied with what he'd offered her.

He swallowed. Molly, on the other hand, hadn't asked him for a damn thing.

And that was exactly what he'd given her. Nothing.

He'd expected her to change her whole life for him. And when she'd blinked, what had he done? He'd stormed out of there without giving her a chance to think, without giving them a chance to come up with a solution.

But that was about to change.

If she'd have him back.

He loved her, dammit. If she felt the same way, they *could* work something out.

He knocked the back of his head against his plane's fuselage a couple of times. If he hadn't already screwed this up completely, that was. His eyes searched out the next number on his list and flipped open his cellphone, turning to face the plane for privacy. The dial tone gave way to ringing once he finished punching in the buttons. He waited a second or two.

"You promised to teach me to fly."

"Hello?" His mind went deadly still when he realized the voice hadn't come from his phone, but from somewhere behind him. He shook the instrument just to make sure, then put it back to his ear. Still ringing.

"Blake."

He knew that voice. Clicking the phone shut, he turned around slowly, expecting to see empty space. Instead, his gaze fell on the person who'd driven him to call every major hospital in the United States looking for another Care Flight job.

Molly. Green eyes shining, something gripped between her fingertips. The apparition took a step forward.

"I'm sorry?" He had to be sure he wasn't trapped in some kind of stress-generated delusion.

"I said, you promised to teach me to fly." Her hand came up, holding a small plastic case. He recognized his computer simulation game. "I should buy my own copy, though, so I don't have to keep borrowing yours."

"You want me to teach you to fly?" He drew a careful breath. "Why?"

She licked her lips, a hint of hesitancy behind her eyes now. "I've decided to stay on the island. Or go back to Alaska Regional if my contract isn't renewed. Either way, I'll be doing a lot of flying back and forth."

"What about Gary? You said you couldn't go back because of him."

"I know, but I've spent my whole life trying to avoid conflict, trying to keep the peace. First between my parents as I was growing up, then in my relationships as an adult. When I couldn't avoid conflict, I backed away from it. I've never run *toward* anything in my life." She looked at him. "Until now."

A rush of moisture gathered behind his eyes, and he tried to force it back. "Are you sure this is what you want?"

"It is. I love you. I want to be wherever you are, or as close as I can get." A frown appeared. "Unless you don't feel the same?"

"I do." He held up his list with a laugh. "I've racked my brain trying to remember all the hospitals you had in that folder of yours, and I've been calling every single one of them, looking for a job."

"You have? That's just…" She closed the space between them. "I'm sorry, Blake. I should have told you about the letters. It just seemed so far off at the time. And I didn't want to make waves."

"It's okay. All I want to know is one thing. Did you mean what you said?"

"About staying on the island?"

"No. The other thing."

"Yes. I meant it." The merest trace of a pause. "I love you."

"Thank God." He hauled her against him and kissed her with everything he had in him.

When they finally broke apart, she pulled in a couple of quick breaths. "Does that mean what I think it does?"

"Yes, I love you, too."

She leaned against him, her arms going around his waist. Everything in his world righted itself at her touch.

Unable to resist, he bent down to kiss her again, a melding of mouths and spirits that held the promise of a bright future. "Can you handle living on an island and being involved with a pilot? If not, I can change. Do anything you want me to do."

"All I want you to do is come back to Unalaska with me."
She paused, tightening her arms. "When Sammi told me you'd
left, I panicked. Wondered if I'd ever see you again."

"Mark knew where I was."

She smiled. "I know. He's the one who helped me find
you."

"Remind me to thank him." This time there was no jeal-
ousy involved. Only a grateful heart. Maybe there was hope
for his friend after all.

"I will, once we get back." She pressed a kiss to the underside of his jaw.

"Sure you don't want to stay here for a few days?"

"I'm sure. I just want to go home."

He stroked his fingers down the side of her face. "Even
though it means we have to fly?"

"That's why I brought the program with me." She let go
of him long enough to glance at the case she still held in her
hand. "I know how much you love your job. I want to be a
part of it. That means facing my fears instead of running
from them."

His heart threatened to burst out of his chest. "We'll work
on it. Whether it takes twelve steps or two thousand, I'll be
there."

"That's good, because you never know. If something happens, I might just need to find us a safe place to land."

He smoothed her hair back from her cheeks and leaned in
for another kiss. "I think we're already there."

* * * * *

CAP